SELECTED SHORT STORIES

By the same author

FICTION
The Blue Bed
The Water Music and Other Stories
The Valley, the City, the Village
The Learning Lark
The Island of Apples

VERSE
Poems
The Dream of Jake Hopkins

ESSAYS
The Dragon has Two Tongues

TRANSLATION
The Saga of Llywarch the Old
(with Dr. T. J. Morgan)

Newport Libraries

THIS ITEM SHOULD BE RETURNED OR
RENEWED BY THE LAST DATE
STAMPED BELOW.

STACK

27. NOV 00

16. DEC 00

Please return this item to the library from which it
was borrowed   3/2a

SELECTED SHORT STORIES

by

GLYN JONES

LONDON · J M DENT & SONS LTD

(F Jones)

First published in this collection 1971

© 'Jordan', 'The Boy in the Bucket', 'It's not by his Beak you can
Judge a Woodcock', Glyn Jones 1971

Made in Great Britain
at the
Aldine Press · Letchworth · Herts
for
J. M. DENT & SONS LTD
Aldine House · Bedford Street · London

Published with the support of the
Welsh Arts Council (Cyngor Celfyddydau Cymru)

23878

ISBN 0 460 03968 7

CONTENTS

ER SERCHUS GOFFADWRIAETH
AM
DAVID TYDFILYN JONES

ACKNOWLEDGMENTS

The first four stories in this volume, 'Knowledge', 'Wil Thomas', 'Eben Isaac' and 'Cadi Hughes', first appeared in *The Blue Bed*, published by Jonathan Cape in 1937.

'The Saviour', 'The Four-loaded Man', 'An Afternoon at Ewa Shad's', 'Wat Pantathro', 'The Last Will', 'Price-Parry', 'Bowen, Morgan and Williams' and 'The Water Music' first appeared in *The Water Music*, published by George Routledge & Sons in 1944.

The author wishes to thank the Welsh Arts Council (Cyngor Celfyddydau Cymru) for its generous financial assistance in the publication of this volume.

KNOWLEDGE

On the top of Ystrad Pit three men were repairing the winding rope which raised and lowered the cage in the shaft. It was a lovely sunny morning, blue and fresh, and they worked with the thick black criss-cross shadows of the steel winding-gear falling across them over the sparkling ground, and their fire looking pale because of the strong sunlight, as though it were going out. One of the men was the colliery smith, a grey priest-like old man with a serious, almost mournful, expression, gentle, having the face of one possessing himself completely, claiming nothing. He was grey and clean-shaven, dressed in an old cotton boiler suit of navy blue, and he wore a soiled cap with the peak broken in the middle above his eyes. But although he was old, and his eyes were weary, his body was slim and upright, and the grip of his hands on the stubborn rope was vigorous, as assured and masterful as the handling of a young man; but his face wasn't masterful at all, only kindly and gentle with knowledge.

The three of them, the two men and the boy, were working at the pithead and not speaking much, with the cage hitched up in safety above them near the sheaves, and the arm-thick steel rope lying coiled over the dusty ground at their feet. They had the stiff brush of strands from its ravelled end fixed securely up like spiky hairs through the bottom of the cappel, the sort of deep iron cup, or inverted bell, held in a bench-vice, into which the second man was pouring molten metal out of a long steel ladle. The boy apprentice, very dirty with grease and coal-dust, was blowing the fire-bucket from time to time with a foot-bellows to keep molten the iron crucible of white metal alloy hanging over it.

The man pouring out the liquid metal was the pit-man, being responsible for the ropes, and the cages, and the shaft of the pit generally, a big handsome youngish man, with grace in him and restraint, doing his delicate job easily and with perfection.

He was using a lipped ladle with a long flat metal handle that he gripped with squares of soft leather, tipping the liquid metal out like water, waiting for it to sink a bit on cooling and then filling it up again to the brim; and he never spilt any, he had done it so often, although once or twice it swelled up like a bubble with the scum cracking on the blister-like curve. He had taken off the oilskins he usually wore for his job and was working in a thin white shirt with his sleeves rolled up almost to his shoulders, and his trousers fastened low about his loins by means of a thick leather belt buckled with two tongues of brass. He was big and powerful, his flesh, like most pit workers', as white as a girl's in the sunlight, and his arms large and white, and solid, but smooth, not lumped into muscle although they looked capable and were firm with power. He wore a wide leather strap on his wrist and his hands were big too and soiled, with blunt fingers. He was much younger than the smith but he effaced him with his huge shapely body and his energy. His face was pale and smooth, rounded, and his soft dark hair was cropped short, not moving in the breeze; he was very big, his thin shirt tight on him, and yet he seemed shy, his light eyes troubled a bit from time to time as though he feared being hurt, although not through the body, and his handsome edgy lips were too ready for kindness. He had none of the smith's gentle stoicism and endurance. He knew he could be hurt and he feared it.

The smith was his father-in-law.

Finally the bell-shaped container was completely filled and the pitman lighted a cigarette, waiting for the metal to cool before fixing the rope back on to the top of the cage. It was Sunday and there were no workmen about the colliery, only one or two officials and the lamp man. The boy, who had not long left school, was trying to pitch his cap over the sparrows.

'When are you coming up?' asked the pitman, speaking to his father-in-law.

'I'll come up some night this week, Penn,' he said, stretching out his hand towards the cooling metal. 'Is Gwyn all right?'

'She's all right,' the pitman answered, 'only wondering when you're coming up.'

The old smith smiled; there was sympathy between the two men.

Gwyn was Penn's wife, being eight or ten years younger than himself, a kind of stranger people didn't know very easily, a bit awkward and distant with anyone she didn't care about. People liked her, she was so pretty, narrow, with long straight yellow hair almost golden, cut in a long bob at the back nearly to her shoulders, and growing cropped in a line across her forehead; and she had white skin and spotted blue eyes. But there was something in her people missed, as though she kept something back purposely for herself from everybody. She wasn't easy in her intercourse with people and she flushed readily, as though speaking to anyone unfamiliar was a strain, a good bit of a hardship. But inwardly she had the steady unassuming assurance of the old smith, her father. She had no real fear of being hurt at all; she disliked irritating little contacts with people and she avoided them, being at times almost panicky, but she was passionate and she knew she could fight although she never wanted to. Penn understood this somehow and he relied on her, feeling safe with her at his back; she put such spunk into him.

When the metal was cool through and through Penn got up the iron ladder on to a platform in the winding-gear high above the open mouth of the shaft that tapered below him like a huge inverted fool's-cap, and clamped the rope on to the cage with two long strips of reddened steel. He watched the spokes of the big wheels above him beginning slowly to move round in answer to his signal, and the thick steel rope dithering like a harp-string as it took the weight of the big iron cage; and then he tested his job himself by getting into his yellow oilskins and being wound down the shaft standing on the roof of the cage. Everything was in order. When he returned to the surface he called to his father-in-law and started up his motor-bike for home.

. . . . .

Penn and Gwyn lived in a pleasant old house belonging to her father, a good way from the pit, right out in the country beyond the edge of the coalfield, with the wooded mountains beginning close behind it. In some ways living there was inconvenient for them because if there was something wrong at the pit Penn had to go out at once, often in the middle of the night and in all weathers, to get to his job somehow. But he had his motor-bike and they thought it was worth it to be out of the dreary shabby town and the smoke and the endless noise. The house was pretty, with the bright-coloured painting Penn had done to the outside woodwork, and all the flowers and the trellises; it stood the other side of a brook with a wooden bridge over it, and it had a big garden at the back with fruit trees and roses.

Penn spent most of his time growing flowers, particularly roses, and in summer he gave away dozens of bunches to his friends. It was queer to watch him in the rose-garden; he had a large number of little white linen tents, that he could adjust against the sun, clipped on to the supporting stakes of his most valuable standard rose-trees; and when he looked at the blooms under them he became intent, as though his eyes were seeing past every curled rose-petal, touching the small inner quick and earth-urge that thrust up the stalk and pushed out the shallow petal wrapping from the tiny yellow attachment to the stem; he looked as though he were seeing all over the flower and into the heart of it, right down the thin trunk-stem, knowing the action of its threaded roots; and his big hands would go delicately into the thick of a rose bush, feeling their way round a flower to pull it back to see the loose rose-whorl of its petals, or to scissor it off low down on the stalk.

When Gwyn saw him stooping to handle the roses, peering into the tangled bushes at them in his intense absorbed way, so quiet, she felt excluded, strangely out of it. She couldn't see she came in there anywhere, but she loved him for it, shearing himself off like that from time and place, caring about nothing, existing only with the rose between his hands and at peace with it. She was filled with tenderness for him almost to tears, seeing all the latent feeling and power of his magnificent body fused down to this intense observation of an unbudding flower, giving himself up without any reserve of doubt or fear. But she could see there was nothing scientific or curious in his expression; he seemed as though he understood pretty well already, and his look wasn't of inquiry at all, or speculation, or even wonder, but just acceptance, and slightly puzzled knowledge. When she saw him like that she was at once filled with pity and tenderness, and she was a bit awestruck as well at the completeness of his withdrawal from everything. She used to say nothing at those times with this awe upon her, but just go back to her house-work again.

It wasn't often she asked him to go to chapel with her. She was religious like her father, and went pretty regularly, although she didn't like the concerts and the tea-parties; she went and hurried back home again as quick as she could, not very sociable. But the evening her father came up after work as he had promised she said, 'Penn, dada and I are going to chapel. Will you come?'

He made a face. 'Oh, I don't know,' he said uneasily. He didn't like to refuse outright because of the old smith.

'Come on,' she said, 'this once. You always like the meetings in the weeknights.'

'Oh, all right,' he answered. 'I've got nothing much to do, I don't mind really.'

So the three of them started out, walking.

It was still daylight when they crossed the wooden bridge outside the house, but the chapel was in the town and by the time they got there it had become quite dark and the lights were lit in the streets. They went through the wooden door into the warm silent little schoolroom behind the chapel where the meeting was to be held. Here they separated, Gwyn going on to sit with the other women near the fire the far side of the aisle between the benches, and the two men finding seats in the recess at the side of the wooden door-porch. They were early and there was hardly anybody there, only half a dozen women and two or three men on the benches near Penn and his father-in-law, and when they sat down there was dead silence, except for the gas coming hoarse through the rusty brackets sticking out of the walls, and the tack-tack of the clock over the fireplace swinging its quick pendulum behind the little glass window. Apart from these noises and the sound from time to time of the slipping fire in the big grate there was a drowsy silence that sank into him throughout the room, very warm and peaceful, and comfortable.

Penn had been once or twice before but it was always a bit strange to him, the shabby schoolroom and the few motionless people waiting absorbed in utter silence for the meeting to begin, because his family was English really and church, and he had gone there when he was younger. He watched the people coming in, one or two at a time, short people nearly all of them, undistinguished, the majority of the men colliers dressed almost invariably in black suits, with their skin pale and shining, looking tight and a bit sickly in the green gaslight. He watched them creaking awkwardly over the bare knotted floorboards into the shabby vestry and sitting round him, crooked and a bit misshapen some of them, with blue scars tattooed across their hands and their tight shiny faces, not picturesque at all, commonplace, but it was a satisfaction to him somehow to be there touching them, with their rich earthiness warming him through. They sat around him in quiet until they were a good number waiting for the meeting to start, motionless most of the time, some with their eyes shut, solid and finished, wanting nothing; they had been hurt often and had suffered, and they looked uncouth, almost monolithic, with no desire in them, only the warm look of knowledge and understanding. They sat so calm Penn envied them, seeing no bitterness in their easy hands and so much acceptance in the look of their bodies and their clean shining faces. And around them all was the still warm atmosphere, rich and getting drowsy, and the gaslight coming green off the distempered walls.

The meeting started with the young minister reading out a hymn. There was a good number of people present for a week-night, perhaps thirty, and Penn enjoyed the meeting, especially the hymn-singing; the voices were rich and the words and music moving. He was glad he had come. Usually he didn't like any religious service, it seemed to be about something else, nothing to do with him at all. But he never said anything to Gwyn; he wanted her to go if she liked it.

Then several people prayed and quoted scripture, and one or two spoke describing their experiences and temptations, a sort of confessional. They were good too, some of them, natural actors and story tellers, humorous even, and full of drama and vivid speech. Penn was filled with admiration for them, and contented. But near the end the young minister asked Gwyn to pray. He was a nice young man, very earnest and hard-working, and Penn liked him, but he was unwilling at once, and apprehensive. He wanted to stop her from doing it, it wasn't fair. It was wrong because Gwyn was passionate and would say things to give herself away kneeling on the floor before them all. But her father just bowed his face slowly and waited in silence with his eyes closed, calm and tender-looking, quite unmoved. Penn didn't know really why he was so angry and unwilling, resisting it so much, except that he was afraid of what she would say to hurt herself before them, and for a moment he hated all these people sitting round her, waiting to hear her reveal herself; it was ugly to him to see them watching the grace of her kneeling body, secretly triumphing over her, hoping to see how her passion would give her away.

She began softly. Penn didn't really know what she was saying. She was kneeling with her head bowed at an empty chair, her long yellow hair hanging down from under her blue cap so that no one could see her face at all. Her words were muffled, and from time to time she stopped, and there was silence, letting in the buzz of the gaslights, and the eating sound of the coal fire, and the awkward little coughs breaking from the other women. Penn was white, watching her over his hands, pale and strained-looking with his lips dry. As long as he was watching her he felt he could defend her and justify her, and hold her somehow in his protective control against all these other people. He was afraid to stop looking at her and thinking about her, willing her passionately to hold out against the bitter strength of her emotion and the words surging in her blood, lending her his strength. He was resentful towards the women near her and his mouth was like fire. He knew how unfair it was to let her kneel down like this; it was cruelty, but he wouldn't let anything happen to her. He could feel rage and strength filling him like a sap rising at the thought of her giving way; he was in a sort of fury, but quiet, knowing she must resist the concentration of so many wills and he didn't want any longer to stop her; she had to go on and complete her prayer in spite of them while he lent her all his strength. He glanced round feeling powerful with anger and protective tenderness.

Then suddenly her body went slack and she began to sob. She faltered in her prayer a bit and finally stopped, her head jerking slowly over the chair. And then her body shuddered with fierce weeping. She couldn't say anything any more and she just knelt and wept helplessly with her fingers spread out over her face and her hanging hair rocking to and fro from under her cap. She was shaking right through her body before them all with uncontrollable weeping, making hardly any sound except little choking cries from time to time that broke loose from the strife of her throat. Penn was helpless, feeling nothing clearly, bewildered and helpless. Slowly she got up and sat on the bench, her face bowed over her lap, her shoulders hunched and the sobs still jerking through her like stabs. The silence and the tension were awful and interminable to Penn, who sat on defeated and hopeless, not even wondering how it was going to end, completely empty.

Then slowly the young minister got up and gave out a hymn

and they sang with spirit, as though Gwyn's crying had released purity into the room. But she sat throughout the singing slowly coming back from her prayer with the subsidence of her passion, and by the time they had finished she was calm again, flushed and red-eyed, but composed, gathering her things together to leave. Penn was dazed, it was all so sudden and so hateful. After the meeting he found himself walking home with her through the streets, shining after the rain, and saying good night to her father; not one of them had spoken a word of what had happened. In the lane that led up to their house he stopped her and said:

'Gwyn, what was the matter?'

She laughed and lifted up his hand and kissed the knuckles of his fingers clasping hers. He sounded so sad and bewildered she had to comfort him. She went close up to him not being able to stop laughing, he sounded so tragic.

'It was nothing, Penn,' she said, 'only I love our people and I so seldom show it. Smell the gillies in the garden after the rain. I am so busy fighting.'

She ran on ahead dragging him by the hand. It all seemed so strange to Penn.

WIL THOMAS

At the top of a disused incline running up the mountain stood a lonely row of ironworkers' cottages. In front of them were fields and rough heathland, but behind, the big black tips rose up into the height of perpendicular cliffs, crested and streaked with white clinker like the droppings of gigantic birds. On the doorstep of the end cottage a man called Wil Thomas stood looking down the incline towards the town in the valley, and watching the sun beginning to set in the clouds beyond as though it were going down behind a sheet of yellow celluloid. He had an empty beer bottle in his hand and he was waiting for his wife to come home from the prayer meeting.

Wil was an ordinary enough chap to look at, being heavy and thick-set, with short legs, wearing a greenish tweed suit and a white muffler. His body was egg-shaped, set diagonally from back to front, with the heavy end of the egg swelling out full behind the lower end of his tight waistcoat and the fly-buttons of his trousers, stretching them apart, and the small end rising in a low hump between his shoulder-blades, lifting out his coat a bit. He had no neck and his head fitted plumb on to his body. His hair was white and cut short, and for a nose he had a hook like a large soft beak, big and fleshy, constellated all over with small equally spaced out blue black-heads like pencil dots. His heavy jaw, wanting a shave, was like white velvet and his eyes were noticeable, being khaki – his eye, more like, because he had only one. The place where the other had been looked sore, the raw lids hanging loose, the flesh all round red as though the eye-hole had been cut in his skin with a scissors. Usually he wore a false eye, but he hadn't had it in for the last fortnight because he had been home from work with a clout on the back, so that he hadn't been able to leave the house at all.

After looking down the hillside for a bit he grinned to himself because he was able to make out his wife struggling up the incline road with her breath in her fist. As she got nearer he could tell by the explosive kind of way she was walking, jerky, automatic, scattering her feet and kicking her skirts out, that she wasn't very sweet; and she wasn't either, although she had been to the prayer meeting. Before going she had put her coms through the mangle and broken the buttons, and that had upset her; and now her feet were beginning to ache and her back-comb was sticking hard into her head under her heavy best hat and giving her jip every yard of the way. And she knew what Wil would be after with his clowning as soon as she got to the house. But she wasn't going until she'd had a rest. He'd have to wait for his beer for once, that was all about it.

When she got up to the doorstep Wil stopped her going into the house and pointed over her shoulder towards the sunset with the flagon. 'Mari,' he said, gazing before him, 'what other hand than His?'

She pushed past him into the kitchen. 'I know what you want,' she snapped. 'As long as you can bathe your gums that's all you care about.'

Will shrugged his shoulders, grinning to himself. He was a bit of a comic and he thought he would be able to humour her saying something like that. But she was a queer plant. She could be awkward when she wanted to, Wil knew that, turning very spiteful and touchy at times. She was a little woman dressed in a big heavy hat of black velvet and a dark costume with long wide skirts, and she had little steel glasses on only just big enough to cover her eyes, with black darning wool wound round the nose-piece. She was always full of quick mechanical energy, her movements were always a bit sudden and automatic-looking, and now, because of her boots and her heavy hat, she was filled up with spite and malice, vindictive, as fierce and quarrelsome as a little bullfinch. Her face was a bit purpler than usual, and her small tidy little features looked snappish, disgusted with everything, and her lips were tight too, and hard as a couple of pebbles, evil-looking. But Wil wasn't a bit frightened by her nasty little darting eyes or the sharp looks she kept on giving him as he followed her about carrying the empty bottle. He only grinned behind her back and after a lot of coaxing he got her to go for the beer. She put a tin of steak and onions to cook slowly in the oven for him and then went out wearing comfortable things, old shoes and a shawl, and one of his cast-off caps on her head. She wasn't willing but she couldn't refuse him somehow.

'Well done, little Mari,' he said, and he came with her to the doorstep. 'You'll think of this in years to come. Long after I have joined my eye, my little pelican.'

He grinned after her as she went back down the hill to the village.

Soon it began to get dark in the house so Wil lit the oil lamp and put it on the table by the window. Then he pulled the blind down and sat by the fire feeling pretty good, taking an occasional look at Mari's medicine bottle that was standing on the window-sill, and enjoying the warmth and the steak and onions smell coming strong from the oven, listening from time to time to the wind outside beginning to rise over the mountains, moving uneasily in the belly of the darkness. His bad back was comfortable too, and he was enjoying himself fine by the fire in his low little kitchen, dreaming about his eye, which had dropped out like a pop-alley when he was born, or had been eaten by a rat that time he was dull enough to work underground, he couldn't remember which, he had told so many different tales about it. No, that was sure to be wrong though, he wasn't any rat's leavings, he was sure of that. He had dug a fork into it when the woman next door ran out of the lavatory on fire, that was more like it. Yes that was it, she was Lisa Richards, number two, who used to smoke her husband's long-ends in the lavatory, but what she'd done was set herself on fire by accident the wicked bitch and made Wil stick an old fork in his eye with excitement. But he felt pretty good waiting for Mari to come home with the beer.

Then the preacher knocked at the door.

'*Uffern gol's*,' said Wil, 'who can be there now?'

He got up and went to have a look, taking the lamp off the

table with him because it had become quite dark outside. When he saw it was Evans he brought him in at once. 'Come on in, come on in,' he said, glad of company now that he had been feeling so shabby. 'Damn it all, little Evans, come on in at once.' The preacher stepped from the pavement into the kitchen, ducking as he came, thanking Wil in his big preaching voice.

'May the thumbs of the dragon never lift the latch of William Thomas,' he said in his big voice, stopping just inside the door, towering above Wil with his hand aloft. 'How do you feel, William?'

'Blessèd, little Evans,' said Wil, 'blessèd. Come right in and sit your little bottom down on the stool over by here.'

Evans was a queer-looking chap, tall and dark, dressed from head to foot in black clothes, having his mouth half-way up his face and filled with big false teeth that were broken in the plate and rattled when he was talking like a pocketful of taws. He had big nostrils too with tufts of black hairs sticking out of them, hooked and black like little bunches of candlewicks. He always wore very thick glasses that made his black boot-button eyes look small and queer, with the glass in them as thick as a pop bottle, and his eyebrows were heavy and black, curving upwards, the shape of nail-parings.

'Come right over here by the fire,' said Wil, noticing his funny strong smell. And when he had got him sitting he took his black hat off for him so that his ears sprang upright, and then he hung it on his knee. The preacher's forehead was the width of a good garter and his hair was like astrakhan.

Wil never went to chapel himself, he pretended he was too dense, but he wasn't embarrassed at all because of that. He was glad to have Evans in the house, hoping to be able to tease him a bit, because the preacher was supposed to be a bit simple, and once he had cocked his leg over the pulpit to show the people Balaam riding on the donkey. But he wanted to make him feel at home as well.

'Have a cup of tea?' he said.

'No tea,' said Evans, shaking his face.

'Small beer then?' said Wil.

'No small beer,' said Evans.

'Whisky and water?' said Wil, moving towards the window-sill.

'No water,' said Evans, and he sucked a line of fluid like a macaroni pipe back up into his nose.

Wil was glad he had shown willing anyway. He got down two cups and poured out the whisky from the medicine bottle Mari kept on the window-sill for her heartburn, and they enjoyed themselves nice and tidy. They sat at the table in the low comfortable little kitchen, one each side of the lamp, with Wil's nose throwing a huge shadow shaped like a rudder across his face and Evans turning his eyes up and muttering as the whisky was coming out of the bottle. Wil did most of the talking at first, he was glad to, living in that back-crack up the incline and not being able to go out at all, but he was watching Evans all the time, trying to draw him out. He started to talk about the compo doctor not asking him how he felt but how soon he was going to start work again, and then he spat in the fire with disgust.

'There is none to hold up the arms of the needy, William,' said Evans, solemn and important, and he drew up through his nose again so that he could have a drink. His big face near the lamp-globe was full of edges under his thin skin, and heavy looking, with a lot of bone in it like a horse.

'There's no two ways about that,' said Wil, convinced. 'How are you shaping? Aren't you empty yet?'

Evans glanced down into his cup. 'The lord giveth and the lord taketh away,' he said, gazing at the ceiling boards as Wil poured out again.

And with a new drink in front of him, and Wil encouraging him, he cleared his throat and started to talk, letting Wil have one of his old sermons, the one about Samson and Delilah and the Dragon. 'Like me,' said Wil, interrupting him for devilment and wiping his eye with his coat-sleeve, 'I dug a fork in mine.'

Evans swallowed with a lot of noise, a bit impatient, wanting to get on. 'The scratches of the Dragon are stripes in the army of the lord,' he said, heavy and dramatic, starting off again.

'Quite right, quite right, little Evans,' Wil broke out showing he was convinced, and nearly upsetting his whisky. 'And when I'm in the bar of the Angel and I want to pass water, Evans, I haven't got to spit in my beer before I go out, see?' Evans nodded slowly, not very interested, anxious to have his own say. 'I've only got to take my glass eye out,' Wil went on acting the part, 'and put it on the counter by my pint and everything is fine. I only say, "Watch here a bit, little one", and it's as good as if I was there myself.' He picked up his cup and held it to his lips grinning. 'That's quite right what you said, little Evans.'

Wil took a sip. But Evans waved his big hands before his face eager to have another go. He looked cunning and while Wil was swallowing his drink he took his chance and started off again.

'It is better to have one eye, William,' he said, 'than two and hell fire . . .'

Wil brought his cup down smartly. 'There was hell fire when I lost mine all right,' he broke out in a hurry, and then he went on describing and acting how he had been on the back doorstep getting a cork out of a bottle with a fork when the woman next door ran out into the garden on fire.

'The roots of the tobacco tree are suckled in hell below,' said Evans, poking his finger out at Wil with his thumb up like a trigger, determined to be listened to, 'but I have come to speak comfort, William, if my arm is long enough. I ought to have said my tongue, that was a mistake.' He boomed at Wil and lifted the lamp towards him. 'I have brattice, William, against the blowings of the Dragon. I can make you a whole man again.'

Wil grinned at him, thinking he'd got him well started now. 'That's how you chaps are when you wear your collars arse-frontwards,' he said, 'you'll say anything.' He just leaned back and let Evans have his say, preparing to enjoy himself.

But what fascinated him after a bit was the preacher's nose.

He was so interested he couldn't take his eyes off it. One of the huge black nostrils had dried up in the heat and left a narrow glistening line like a snailtrack along his upper lip between his nostril and his mouth; but the other side was exciting to watch because it was still active, and a thin tube of whitish liquid was all the time creeping slyly out of his nose and advancing towards his mouth as he was talking. At times Will got so excited he could hardly hear what he was saying, thinking the snot would tap him on the knee or the back of the hand, but always at the last minute Evans would sniff it up again out of sight. Then Wil would listen in comfort for a bit until it began to signal once more, wet and shiny among the growth of black hairs.

He was so excited and amused, most of what Evans was getting on about was going right over his head and he didn't notice how he was working himself up. The chap was talking like the river, his broken teeth chattering as though there was a horse-bit in his mouth and his arms were exercising in front of his face like mad. Then he stood up suddenly, still talking in his double bass, and his hat fell off his knee to the rag rug, but he took no notice of it at all. Instead he stood towering above Wil in his black clothes with his glove-back hair up against the planks of the ceiling and his huge shadow flapping about on the wall like a big bat's umbrellas or the wings of a goody-hoo. Wil was a bit surprised at first, thinking it funny that the medicine was making him talk like this, but wishing all the same he'd go off the boil a bit and take it easy now before Mari got back.

'Little Evans, little Evans,' he said trying to soothe him, 'sit down and be comfortable and don't stand up there, boy, bending like a bluebell.' But Evans took no notice, and because of something or other he'd said he started emptying the tail pocket of his frock coat, babbling all the time about the dragon and taking things out of his pocket by the fistful, piling them on the table in the round pool of lamplight. 'Well God knows,' Wil grinned to himself, 'there was supposed to be everything in the ark but there's sure to be more in this.'

Evans went on talking as fast as he could, with his pointed Adam's apple working like a piston, but he wasn't getting any change out of Wil although he continued being dramatic, pulling things out of his pocket, string and papers and pins and camphor balls. 'No doubt that's why he always smells like the cathedral,' thought Wil wondering what was coming out next. And because the preacher looked as though he was going to tread on it, he picked up his hat off the rug for him and put it under the lamp, where it looked, because of the dent across the top, like the round head of a big black screw driven into the table.

When he looked up again Evans had brought a human eye out of his pocket.

'Wonderful man,' cried Wil jumping up, forgetting all his clowning, 'what's that you've got there?'

It was a real eye, fresh and glistening in the lamp-light, with threads of thin steam rising from it and the nerve-roots hanging out between the preacher's fingers. It lay solid and big as a fine peeled egg, shining among the camphor balls on his shaking palm, polished like china in the lamplight, with the pupil and the khaki iris gazing up at Wil in a fixed way he didn't like at all. There were no lids on it, and it stared wickedly up at him all the time so that he couldn't avoid it whichever way he looked, fixing its clear shining pupil on his good eye, making him feel very uneasy; and although there was no face round it it seemed to be jeering at him all the time. He had seen plenty of scraps of bodies about after accidents in work, and when he was a boy he had carried the top of the lodger's finger about in a match-box until it stunk too bad, but he had never seen anything like the eye before. He couldn't have touched it for a fortune although Evans was holding it out to him, asking him to take it, his arm going up and down under Wil's face like a pump handle. And he began to look so fierce, he was turning so curly that Wil thought he'd better take it into his hand to save trouble. It was cold and wet underneath, slimy like a peeled plum, heavy and moist as an egg-plum with the skin pulled off as the juices of the chilly wet flesh touched his unwilling palm.

Will shivered from head to foot, and outside the loud wind stumbled over the house.

As Mari was coming up the dark lonely incline in the wind, carrying the beer, she said good night to some man she wasn't sure of. He reminded her of Evans the minister. 'Poor fellow,' she thought, 'a year ago to-day he swam the Jordan.'

When she got back to the house the lamp had burnt out, and when she relit it she saw Wil lying on the sofa fast asleep on his back, and looking pretty rough. She went through a little door into the pantry to put the beer on the stone, and when she came out she noticed her whisky bottle was empty on the window-sill. That settled her. Without stopping to take off her things she pulled Wil's steak and onions out of the oven and ate them up with relish, while Wil still lay fast asleep with his mouth open on the sofa behind her. Then she drank his beer. The gravy that was left over in the tin from the steak and onions she spread around his mouth, where it stuck well because he hadn't shaved for a few days. Then she took out a book called the *Grapes of Canaan* and, adjusting her little steel glasses, sat by the fire reading. Her face was innocent, white, round as a little coin.

At last Wil woke up. He wanted his beer. 'Mari,' he said, 'let me have my supper.'

'Supper,' she snapped at him, 'how many suppers do you want, you belly-dog?' She snatched the looking-glass off the wall and held it before his face.

Wil clapped his hand to his empty eye.

EBEN ISAAC

Pentrebach was a little farming village in the hills behind the Sidan bay, a couple of rows of whitewashed cottages in a street sloping up to the top of a hill where there was a square with a pump in it. From here you could see the cut fields on the hills all round like sheets of green blotting paper surrounded by the black cables of the hedges, and on a clear day you could make out the sea, smooth as a slab of blue bag-leather in the distance.

The village baker was a mean old man called Eben Isaac Evans, a slow-moving silent old creature who was always grousing and belching about in the darkness of his little cellar of a bakehouse. In appearance he was a bit of a peasant, heavy and thick in the body, full-shouldered, but with legs so short you couldn't stand a two-foot rule upright between them to the fork of his trousers. His bald head was shiny and tight as a plum-skin, and he had a noticeable turn in his left eye which looked like a horse-ball because the coloured iris was tucked up almost out of sight in the corner; then swelling full out of the middle of his pale shrunken face was a thick fleshy nose, inflamed and veiny, like the rubber bulb of a water pistol or a barber's spray bottle. Often you could see him standing motionless by the bakehouse oven with a brine-bead hanging under it.

He wasn't very handsome, what with his bad eye and his drooping moustache that was like a scarce fringe of yellow cottons hanging out of his lip, but he was married all the same. He lived with his wife Keziah, a loud-mouthed blowzy woman, next door to the bakehouse, right on the main village road, and it was on this road that Keziah spent most of her time; she stood there watching the funerals coming down the street on their way to the graveyard outside the village. Every time one of these processions came in sight she made Eben Isaac come up out of the bakehouse with his bowler hat on so that he could take it off as the body passed the door; and she always used to shout to the men carrying the bier to find out who was being buried, even when she knew all about it already. Sometimes the mourners who knew about her would tease her, and once, as Eben Isaac was standing beside her in his shirt-sleeves, hat in hand, he heard her call out, 'Dafy Etwart, whose corpse have you got there?'

'Shadrach,' answered the bearer, 'the husband of Mari the Bag.'

'Oh, he's a heavy one. Have you carried him all the way?'

'No indeed, little Keziah, he walked for us as far as the pump.'

She grunted as the other bearers laughed, and spat a spider on to the dusty road.

It was funny she had to ask so many questions because according to her she used to see the ghost-candles in the street at night, the spirit-funerals meaning somebody was going to pass away pretty soon. But nobody took much notice of her with her noise and her shouting. She was fat and dirty, tent-like, with her black clothes sloping out all round from her neck-band; and because she never wore her stays her breasts hung down inside her thin black blouses like a pair of huge buttons hanging off, drooping loosely right over the tapes of her swelling sack apron. She never had her false teeth in, and she wore her hair on top of her head in a loose bun, balanced there in the shape of a horse-tod. She was always worth seeing stand-ing on the top step of the bakehouse in her dirty white canvas shoes, cleaning the dirt out of her nails with a hairpin, or coming untidy out of the house before breakfast, scratching her jaw and showing all her empty red gums as she yawned at the morning.

One day in the summer Griff Penclawdd was killing a bull in his farmyard just outside the village, and everybody from Pentrebach had gone down to see it. It was a lovely sunny day, the fresh whitewash on the cottages was bright and flat as marble in the brilliant sunshine, and the tree growing out of the top of Eben Isaac's chimney was throwing a black basketwork shadow down on to the road. But the village itself was deserted, and the white pigeons were down like clockwork in the street after grain and the indian-corn. Keziah had gone with the others, but she had made Eben Isaac stay behind to work down in the black sweltering bakehouse. He stood for a long time after she had gone without moving, patiently waiting near the iron oven door for the bread to do, his shrunken face lit up beside the elbowed bat's-wing burner that was the only bit of light in the black bakehouse; he was in his shirt-sleeves, covered right down to the eye-holes of his boots with flour, and in his hand he held the tall wooden oar he used for shovelling the bread-tins out of the oven.

From time to time his hollow cheeks filled out with wind like puffy sails as he belched gently to himself, but apart from that he did not move at all. He stood still there so long the arm he was holding the bread-pole with began to go to sleep and he thought drowsily to himself, 'No, my arm is wide awake, I can feel it, it's the rest of me must be going to sleep'. He was always a bit dull and while he was puzzling which it was, he heard the sound of gritty cartwheels rumbling down the road in the distance, crunching over the small stones of the street outside with a noise at last like the hissing sound of a scissors scissoring through a cut of thick hair.

He walked over to the little square window, lifted the flour sack off the rusty nail, and looked out blinking into the sunny street. His chin behind the dusty glass, because the bakehouse had been built sunk below the roadway, was about on a level with the pavement pebbles. As he crossed the flagstones of the bakehouse floor to the window he noticed from the thumping noise that the tip of his left boot was missing.

There was nobody in the street when he put his face against the pane, but in a minute or two Steffan the Smelly came into sight wheeling his fish-cart. And on it he had an elm coffin with white metal handles like door-knockers. Eben Isaac lifted his dusty bowler without thinking from the hook behind the door, put it on and went up blinking out of the bakehouse to the top step, carrying his long oven-oar with him. He watched

Steffan hanging back on the shafts of the cart because of the slope, and he got ready to call out to him. 'Steffan,' he shouted from the street doorstep when the cart was opposite, 'whose body have you got there?'

Steffan spent most of his time tramping about the country, being always on somebody's knocker for the end of the loaf, or a slice of bacon fat, but sometimes he sold fish among the hills from a handcart. He had three bowler hats on his head and two beards. One of the beards was a thick little tuft of hair stuck in the middle under his lower lip like a hairy beech-nut that moved independently when he was talking, and the other was a thick, coco-nut, lion's-mane of bull's wool wrapped round his neck and half his face. The skin of his broad nose was about the only bit of face-flesh he had in sight, and that, curving out into the sunshine from beneath the shadow of his hats, was full of small holes like a piece of orange peel. Then at the base of his nose, just where the nostril joined on to the cheek, he had a yellow growth like a shrivelled green pea that he used to play with when he was thinking. He had on a long black overcoat of some curly stuff, reaching almost to his heels and fastened in the middle with a six-inch safety-pin. His right boot had no tongue, and was cut from the lace-holes half-way across the toe-cap, showing his green woollen stockings. The other boot fitted better because it came from a different pair.

He took no notice the first time Eben Isaac shouted. So, with his hat still on his chest, Eben shouted again, 'Steffan, who have you got there?'

'Eben Isaac Evans,' Steffan answered, looking puzzled up at the houses, 'the baker of Pentrebach.'

That brought Eben Isaac's eye out of the corner, and the water-drop under his nose began to swing like a sign-board in the wind with the jerk it gave him. But just then, before he could say anything, the front door of the pink house opposite opened and old Harri Hir, a tall white figure, ran out of the shadows into the sunlight shouting, 'Steffan, Steffan, a nice meaty bloater, Steffan,' filling the silent street with his noise

and frightening the pigeons who slapped their little sides with
their wings and rose to the roofs. He was a very long, narrow old
man with a white beard down to his middle, thin, and so blood-
less three fleas could have sucked him dry. He was not wearing
any of his top-clothes when he ran out into the street and he was
dressed only in a cream flannel vest and knee-drawers with
black knitted stockings on his legs with scarlet toes and heels.
He was a queer old man who used to act as a midwife when he
was younger, but he was a bit cracked now and one of his
favourite games during full moon was to stand for hours behind
his front door with his fingers hanging out through the letterbox.

Steffan stopped and old Harri trotted up to the cart, chuckling to himself as he came and stroking his beard with his large
cracked hand as though he had an animal on his chest. 'One
with a hard belly, Steffan,' he said as he got alongside the wheels,
but Steffan shook his head at him. 'No fish to-day, little Harri,'
he said smoothing the coffin, 'I only tickled up a dead-head
this time.'

Eben Isaac could only watch them from the bakehouse step
with the sun in his eyes; and just then Harri's ginger kitten ran
out of the pink-washed house after him and started to reach up
against his leg, playing with the tapes of his drawers that dangled
for tying at the knees; but Harri took no notice of it and began
running his nose along the grooves and joints of the coffin,
asking Steffan whose body it could be then.

'Eben Isaac Evans,' he answered, pushing his growth up with
his thumb, 'the baker of Pentrebach.'

Eben Isaac heard it again, but he only stood dejected on the
top step with his head in his feathers, just looking at them,
wondering what he had better do.

'The baker?' said Harri, standing upright again and looking
surprised. 'He will be straight at last then. But he will have the
burns on his knuckles under the lid of his coffin all the same.'

With that he tucked his kitten up under his armpit and ran
back into the house on his heels with his legs stiff, chuckling to
himself and shutting the door with a bang behind him.

Steffan looked after him and shrugged his shoulders, and turned back his coat sleeves that had come down over the backs of his hands. He kicked away the stone he had guided before the cart-wheel and went on, taking no notice of Eben Isaac who began to follow him without thinking down the empty sunlit street. Eben Isaac remembered the burns on the backs of his hands. When he was small and his father had the bakehouse, the apprentice boys who were older than him used to drop ha'pennies into the hot bread tins for him to snatch out, because they knew how much he liked a bit of money even then. His father used to tell him what a good boy he was for doing it.

Presently they left the village and were out on the road leading to the cemetery. The grass on the hedge-banks on both sides was shining like tin in the clear sunlight, and Eben Isaac noticed the big shadow of a bird drop solid as a black stone down the sloping bank on one side, skid slowly across the flat road and bolt suddenly up the opposite slope like something plucked quickly upwards with a string. The bird was a big white gull battering the upper wind, her wings bent like bike-bars. He looked all round on the red road but he found he had no shadow at all in any direction. He belched a bit at that and put his bowler hat on, changing the pole over to the other shoulder. He began to wish his legs were a bit longer because every now and then he had to break into a little trot to keep up with Steffan's cart which was making a noise ahead of him like grit between the teeth, except when it went rubber-tyred over a drying trail of brown cow-stars.

But presently they came round the bend upon Griff Penclawdd's farm, where the road was so narrow you could spit across, and the crowd from the village was making plenty of noise there. On the left-hand side rose the high stone wall of Griff's orchard, and on the top of it a row of farm-boys were sitting to have a good view of the slaughter, mimicking people in the crowd the other side of the road and shouting out rude things to them all the time like, 'Maggie, what did you leave your husband for? To have a drop of titty off your mother?'

or 'Two ounces of cheese please, Hannah the Gwalia, and my mother said to cut it with the bacon knife.'

The farmyard where Griff was going to kill the bull was on the other side of the road from the orchard and here the crowd was gathered, mostly women in shawls and aprons, talking out loud together and looking over the low farm wall into the yard, hiding from view almost everything that was inside except the top of Griff's bald head, orange-coloured, shining with sweat like a piece of brass in the sunlight. Keziah was there for one on the edge of the road, a black cone with her arms folded over her chest and her bun coming down. And the crowd was spread out into the road so much that Eben Isaac was forced to pass near the wall on the other side; and looking up he could see the soles of the farm-boys' boots right above him, the square-headed nails of their big working boots polished as their feet dangled in a row along the wall, and threw a wide fringe of shadows sideways across the stonework.

One of the boys had a glittering piece of mirror in his lap that he was using to tease Griff with, flashing the sunlight, Eben Isaac could tell by the shouting, right across the road into the bull's eyes, and then blazing it bang into Griff's own eyes as he turned round swearing at the top of his voice at whoever was doing it. Eben Isaac could see the long firm beam of bright light coming through the dust Steffan's frayed trousers were kicking up, hanging over the backs of his heels as he walked along; and, just as they passed below the wall, the boy swivelled the shaft of light off the mirror in Eben Isaac's direction, and he saw the beam pass right through him, through the tweed and the buttons of his dusty waistcoat and straight through his body as though he wasn't there at all. And nobody took any notice of him with his missing tip thumping along the road, and the ten-foot bread-shovel sloped over his shoulder.

Some of the boys shouted to Steffan though, 'Steffan, who have you got there on the fishcart?'

'Eben Isaac,' he answered, 'the baker of Pentrebach. He's dead at last.'

They started shouting at that, 'He didn't have much work dying, he didn't,' and, 'There they go again, those haystacks,' because that's how Eben Isaac used to grumble at his apprentice when he loaded his teaspoon with sugar, and everybody in the village knew about it. And some of them started belching as loud as they could, because the baker was famous for that too; he would do it even when someone respectable was in the bakehouse, like Mrs. Thomas the Bank who had a piano and two fireplaces in the parlour. Then just as the coffin passed the spot where the bull was fastened inside the yard Eben Isaac could hear the animal beginning to plunge and bellow, rattling at his chains so that the women scattered a bit, and he could see his tail tossed into the air like a bit of old rope. But Keziah, standing there like a drab, didn't move. 'Strike now, little Griff,' she shouted, 'you'll have a foot more beef,' and all the people laughed, seeing what was happening inside the yard.

Soon they were on their way to the cemetery once more, the cart-rims making a noise in front like a horse tearing grass off a field with his teeth. As they went along Eben Isaac was looking at the rip lengthening the vent of Steffan's overcoat half-way up his back, when suddenly a swallow came lurching swiftly towards him in the dazzle of the sun, licking out its wings along the middle of the road. He ducked when the white breast was flung up near his face but the bird-beak hit him straight between the eyes and went on through his brains without stopping. He sweated, but after a bit got used to it, and he didn't even jump when the blackbirds hurdled the hedges together and went into him and right through him like a broadside.

Then they came in sight of a ploughed field looking like a piece of a big rasp between the hedges, and it was here they had to turn into the little round cemetery. It was neglected, full of tall grass and gravestones, with a day's washing hanging out to dry on a rope across it. Steffan went in and drew the cart up right out in the middle beside a deep open grave, and then he took off his overcoat and laid it across a flat tombstone. Underneath the coat there was a wide space between the top of his trousers and the bottom of his waistcoat, and his right arm was naked because he had ripped out his shirt-sleeve at the shoulder so that he could tickle for trout. For a bit he sat down on his overcoat playing with the growth at the side of his nose and drawing his fingers like a comb through his beard, talking to himself all the time about how he was going to get the coffin down into the hole single-handed. For the first time Eben Isaac was near enough to notice the strong fish-smell coming from the cart, and he was staring at the coffin, thinking how much like tin and cardboard it looked, when he heard Steffan call out, 'Lewsin, Lewsin, come and give us a hand will you?'

Lewsin Parc-y-lan was going by on the other side of the low graveyard wall with a lemon handkerchief round his neck and a double-barrelled shot-gun under his arm. He was a tall thin chap with huge lumpy shoulders and long slender legs, bandy as a pair of cartshafts, that looked thinner because of his tight black corduroy trousers and the big naily boots he always wore. He had gold ear-rings, a huge bunch of oily curls under the peak of his cap and a chin like a rock-cake with smallpox. He got a living by poaching and liming the river. He was a bad character, drinking and fighting about the place, and once he had been living in tally with a gipsy. He got over the stone stile that was on that side of the graveyard when Steffan called him, making a lot of squeaking noises with his naily boots.

'Give us a hand to get this coffin underground will you, Lewsin?' Steffan said again, his beech-nut bobbing about. 'It's Eben Isaac, the baker of Pentrebach.'

'Eben Isaac is it?' said Lewsin, leaning his gun against an angel. 'I don't mind helping to bury a kite like that, I don't. When did he die with you then?'

'Stop you a bit now,' said Steffan pondering, 'if he had lived till next Thursday he'd have been dead a fortnight.' Lewsin grinned; his face was the red of a flowerpot and he showed his long wet teeth, brown as if he had been drinking iodine. He knocked upwards at the coffin bottom with his knuckles where it stuck out over the edge of the cart.

'Jeez, his behind will soon be out of this,' he said. 'He was too mean to give himself a good coffin, was he?'

'Aye, he was,' said Steffan, 'and him with plenty, never giving so much as a red penny to a man and cutting off the dough hanging over the edges of the people's tins for Keziah to make loaves out of it, so they are saying about him in the village then.' They took up the tapes that were ready on a flat gravestone near by and after spitting on their hands they twisted them through the tin door-knockers and lifted the coffin with difficulty off the cart. They carried it to the mouth of the grave and then rested it on the grass, surprised at the weight.

'He's heavier than he looked for such a little runt as him,' said Lewsin, stooping down to read the big tin medal on the coffin-lid with a frown, and rubbing his hands on the seat of his corduroys. 'It doesn't say he was a deacon with them, Steffan,' he said.

'No indeed,' Steffan answered, 'his wife is such a slut she never brushes his bowler hat and there is flour in the brim every Sunday on the chapel hat-rack. They are telling that is why he is not a deacon.'

They lifted the coffin once again together and started lowering it into the grave, Lewsin standing on one side and Steffan on the other. It was heavy and they had a big struggle with it, the muscles on Steffan's bare white arm standing out like ropes. And as it descended by jerks and bumps out of the sunshine, Eben Isaac, standing unnoticed near the head of the hole, could see Steffan's pile of bowler hats slipping forward gradually over his forehead, sliding gently down over the sweat of his forehead as the coffin got lower and lower into the rich red earth. Steffan himself could feel it too, and he tried to jerk them back, but that only made it worse, and the three hats went on creeping up at the back of his head and down over his eyes, threatening to overbalance into the grave. Just as they were nearing his nose, almost on the brink of falling, Steffan flicked off the tapes with a yell and clutched at the brims with both hands, forcing them back on his head again.

The coffin fell crashing down into the grave and Lewsin, his hands still twisted in the tapes, dived in after it and disappeared completely out of sight, thundering down on top of the coffin with a roar like the sound of blind-linen suddenly rolled up. But he was all right, because presently Eben Isaac could hear him cursing out of the deep earth and Steffan, standing on the lip of the grave, began pointing down and cursing back at him; but when Lewsin climbed out, dirty and capless, and ran to the angel's thigh where the blue barrels of his gun were shining, Steffan backed off and suddenly turned and dashed away, howling among the long grass and the tombstones; he fled screaming for cover behind the line of washing, making for the gate, sheltered at last by the sheets and the blankets, a large patch like a pale butterfly prominent on the behind of his trousers.

Eben Isaac never liked guns so he ran too, the opposite way, towards the stile, dropping his bread-oar on the graveyard grass. After trotting through a good number of fields he came at last to the garden behind his bakehouse, and here he put back the stones he had kicked out that morning so that his hens could run through and scratch on the sly in Griff's field the other side. Then he climbed over the wall and went up towards the kitchen door. As he was coming into the house this back way he could see Keziah the other end of the dark passage standing like a pouter pigeon on the doorstep with a black woollen shawl over her shoulders.

'My uncle Niclas,' she was shouting, 'whose body have you got there then?'

'Richard Top of the Cross,' a voice answered from the street, and just then Eben Isaac could see the funeral procession passing the front door.

'Is he dead then?' asked Keziah.

'No indeed, my girl,' her uncle answered, 'to-day is only the rehearsal.'

Eben heard the people laughing as he crept upstairs quietly and went to bed, examining first the heel of his boot where the tip was missing. Then he fell asleep almost at once. When he woke up it was dark in the bedroom except for two candles, one burning on a green cake-plate each side of his head; and he could see a little pane smashed in the window to let the soul out, and a poker leaning upright on the sill. But he wasn't surprised at that at all, nor at the white bedsheets hung all round the walls of the room. He was feeling pretty shabby now, his head was sore as a boil and his mouth tasted as though he had a row of pennies on his tongue. Then presently he heard Keziah answering the front door and bringing someone into the house. 'I knew it would be somebody before long,' she was saying in her loud voice. 'The street was full of lights last night, it was. Come up, the corpse is on the planks in the bedroom.'

CADI HUGHES

Upstairs in number one Colliers' Row, Ifan Cariad was dying by inches. People often say 'dying by inches' without really meaning it, but as a description of Ifan it was almost literally true; because his left leg was gangrenous to the knee, and every day for the last week when Cadi his wife went upstairs to dress it and clean it out she found a new hole, sometimes the size of the palm of her hand, in a different part of his leg or the flesh of his foot. Then yesterday two of his toes had come off into her apron. The disease had started as a small piece of bad skin under the ball of the big toe, and it would soon pass upwards over the knee into his thigh; and then, when his whole leg had become putrid, it would separate from the rest of his body at the hip and lie discarded in the bed beside him. But Ifan would probably be dead before then, poor chap, unless a miracle happened.

Most of the time he was lying sog after the dope the doctor was giving him daily to ease his pain. His face in a short time had become yellow as clay and tiny, hardly bigger than a hand, with his nose rising up tight in the middle like a plucked fowl's breastbone. They had cut his hair short for comfort, and it looked like the pile on black velvet or plush, and fitted like a cap on top of his little monkey-face. And he had become so thin that his body lifted up the bedclothes hardly at all. He never was very much but he had shrunk to nothing. For days he hadn't eaten a bite, and all that had passed his lips was the water that Cadi fed him with out of the spout of the teapot. The smell of cooking nearly made his inside jump out of his belly, but one day near the end he whispered, 'Cadi, give me something to eat'.

'Of course, little Ifan,' she said, humouring him, 'what will you have?'

'I'd like some of that dinner I can smell cooking.'

'Oh, you can't have that, little Ifan,' she said, 'that's the ham boiling for the funeral.'

She was like that, always planning and scheming. She did everything possible for him; it suited her. She wouldn't let the district nurse come near, and when she wasn't actually fussing round him she would pray, or sing hymns in the voice she used when there were strangers in the chapel; not the nice modern hymns about Jesus and harps and rest beyond Jordan, but savage old-time stanzas by cracked Welsh poets preoccupied with punishment and corruption. She was wonderful the way she waited on him. But she had nearly killed him with her bossiness during the twenty years of their married life. When Ifan married her she was worth looking at; she wasn't just pretty like so many of the dark little women with heavy bottoms living in the mining villages, she was a beauty, big and straight, with blue eyes and hair the colour of a new penny. Ifan himself was small and dark; he looked wicked, a handful for any boss, the sort that always smells foul air in the pit and sees too much water in the workings quicker than anybody else, and makes trouble among the men generally. He was all there; and he knew the Mabinogion backwards.

As for her, she had no idea of her own beauty. All she wanted was for things to go on smoothly as she planned them. Anything odd, strange, eccentric, she hated like poison. And Ifan was a bit odd, what with his politics and his vegetarianism. He was a hot socialist but if he went on the stump she held herself off from him and gave him hell. And she didn't just stop with her tongue either. Poor Ifan wasn't much of an agitator in his own house; he had to draw his horns in at number one Colliers' Row or he could look out. She was a holy terror, bossing everybody and making arrangements all round, and turning out such a fuss-arse, and so trivial. And yet Ifan couldn't do without her; he was always a bit soft on her, imagining her, because of her hair, like Rhiannon or Blodeuwedd, or goodness knows who. And he could always think with pleasure of their courting days when the village boys going about in groups used to sing after the courting couples strolling up towards the lonelier roads:

Red are the shivvies and red are the hips,
    Hazel nuts are brown;
Two of us climb up the Pandy tips
    And three of us come down.
Hoo!

There were more verses.

It was then he got his nickname. He was really Ifan Hughes, although everybody called him Ifan Cariad, which signifies Ifan the Lover, or Ifan the Sweetheart. He used to tap at the window of her house at night when he was calling for her, and her mother would call out from inside, 'Who is there?'

'Ifan,' he would answer.

'Which Ifan?'

'Ifan the lover of Cadi.'

The neighbours heard, and such a chance for a nickname seemed like a godsend. He became known as Ifan Cariad Cadi, Ifan the lover of Cadi, or Ifan Cariad. But such a name in the village was never taken as a sign of disrespect. Everybody else had a nickname anyway.

Sunday morning, just as it was getting light, Cadi came into the bedroom to see if he was still alive. It was a bitter raw morning with no sun and thick clouds *crêped* like slab rubber over the sky. He was all right, but just as she was going back to bed someone started knocking hard at the front door. Cadi was surprised, it was so early. She leaned over the banister and saw someone standing outside the figured glass panel she had had put in the middle of the door to best her sister-in-law. It was just a big dark shape, she couldn't tell who, although she stood there guessing instead of going to see. She slipped a petticoat over her head and got into a jacket of Ifan's, shouting, 'Who's there?' There was no answer but the knocking started again, louder this time as though it wasn't going to stop in a hurry.

She opened the door.

It was God.

He was tall, dressed in a dirty green tweed suit with patch pockets and leather buttons but not much better than rags. There was a sack pinned round his shoulders, and on his head was a cloth slouch hat with the brim turned down over his eyes. His clothes were so disreputable, and yet he looked big and splendid somehow. His left leg finished at the knee, and he hugged a rough wooden crutch as thick as a bedpost, with some of the bark still on it, not padded at all, and spreading out like petals at the end. His grey beard was long but rather thin, and much of his skin was covered with red blind boils like rivet heads. His face was handsome though; patriarchal and majestic, but a bit seedy, and his hair was on his collar. She knew him all right.

'Let me in, Cadi,' he said. He was her boss.

She did so, and upstairs he went sprightly enough, and straight into Ifan's room. There was chaff on his back and horse-dung on the heel of his boot.

'What do you want with us, little God?' she asked upstairs, rather anxious. He and Ifan were smiling at one another, knowing, as though they had something good up their sleeve.

'I've come for Ifan,' he said, still smiling and hardly looking at her.

Although she half expected it, it was a good bit of a shock to hear him say it straight out like that. 'O little God,' she began, sobbing, 'don't take Ifan; I can't live with my brother, his wife quarrels with me, and I'm too respectable to be a washerwoman or go to the Big House.'

Ifan grinned. He was a bit pinker than he had been, and more arrogant already.

'I must take him all the same,' said God.

He stood his crutch against the commode and sat on the edge of the bed, quite at home, like a preacher. His eyes were cunning and very bright, with the skin drawn in all round as though his visit were a bit of a lark. He took very little notice of Cadi except to glance at her sometimes with his spotted eyes. She had more or less gone to pieces; all her bossiness and importance had got flat. She snivelled and started to whimper again.

'Take my daughter, Esther Cariad,' she moaned, 'she's unemployed and hard for us to keep.'

'A cup of tea before we go, please,' said God. 'No fear,' he continued, 'it's not I'll be coming for her, Cadi.'

Ifan nodded and looked serious.

She hung about whimpering for a bit and then went downstairs almost gladly to make the tea, and when she returned Ifan was sitting on the side of the bed dressing, with his huge bandaged leg hanging over the edge. She set the tray down hurriedly and started off on another tack. 'Little Ifan,' she pleaded, going up to him, 'don't go and leave me, and me so good to you always.'

Ifan looked at God, one leg in his trousers.

'Not so good, Cadi,' he said, putting his saucer down.

'Indeed I have, little God,' she answered reddening, 'you don't know. I've nursed him hand and foot in illnesses and accidents, and pinched myself in the strikes for him and Esther.'

'Ay I know,' he said, 'but what about having the bile on Labour Day, and throwing his Cheap Editions on the fire, and hiding the pennies for the gas so that he couldn't read at night, and keeping him home from his meetings to do the garden? You're a bitch, Cadi.'

She smiled hoping to humour him. 'It was only a bit of fun,' she said; and seeing Ifan in difficulties over some vital buttons she was bound to go and help him.

'Very humorous,' said God. 'Anyway, come on, Ifan, get on my back. Cadi, thank you for the nice tea. We must be shifting.'

She could see they were going in good earnest. She was red and serious again and desperate. 'Don't go,' she cried. 'Ifan, stop. Let me get you a clean nightshirt first, then.'

'Lay off,' said God, 'you'll tip us.'

'Plenty of nightshirts where I'm going,' said Ifan grinning. 'Good-bye, Cadi.'

Downstairs they went, not too badly. When they were in the passage, seeing them going for good and all, Cadi shouted down over the banister, 'Ifan, have you got a clean handkerchief?'

God put him down quickly in the oak chair Cadi had in the passage for fashion and came headlong back upstairs. He swung at her with his crutch and hit her into the corner by the chest-of-drawers. She lay there in a heap without a sound, her mop of hair half down and her false teeth hanging out of her mouth.

God and Ifan hurried out of the house as fast as they could go, shutting the glass panelled door with a bang behind them.

THE SAVIOUR

The tall swaying girl crouched with her left hand cupped on her lap, digging frantically into the palm of it with the huge fingers of her right hand and blabbing in a husky voice – 'Jesus, let it stop, O Jesus, Jesus, let it stop!'

Outside the sun burned the ground like a famine. The girl felt upon her heart the suffocation of his power, she found no sanctuary for the flesh against his blunted stroke. She bowed her head as it were beneath a scourge, acknowledging his mastery, feeling his ponderous blood-throb pounding heavily like a pulse against the walls of the airless room in which she suffered. Then looking up again into the unfaltering heat with her bulging eyes she began once more to mutter loudly, 'Christ, let it stop, let it stop. O Jesus, let it stop.'

The room where she sat tortured by the outer presences was hung with an inescapable swarm of small and distracting objects, it was confined, oppressive and motionless. She gazed from time to time, her face twisted in growing frenzy, at the uneven wall-paper, drab and plastered with zigzags of eggs and minute flowers, and as her frantic white eyes leapt along the bulges of the walls she felt a sort of anguish, a restless hatred at the sight of the familiar tranquil implements hanging upon their pins and nails, the clothes-brushes and the button-hook, the yawning scissors and the plush pincushion, the gaudy almanacs, the woollen kettle-holder, the circular looking-glass and the little blue book on its loop of twine. She hated them, their constant presence and their incessant signalling to her, she wanted the fiery throb or the thunders of this annihilating sun to consume them at one clap, she felt a demoniac hunger with her own hands to shatter them all in fragments. And then, as her frenzy crested to its peak and her anguished hands cracked against each other, she closed her eyes, seeking a refuge from them in the stupor of the afternoon, and her unrest died within her.

The girl's mother sat rigid some distance in front of the house in the vertical pour of the sunlight, gazing with fixed lids at the workman toiling in her little field. As she sat with her red stick across her knees the dust of the road leading down the naked hill was about her clogged feet. She was tall and heavy, the dusky burden of her flesh borne unstooping upon her loaded bones. Her savage face, the brown skin of it dinted with shallow pock-marks, although peevish and masterful, was beginning to slobber and to lose its formal solidity, the lower half of it sagged like softening brown rock gone flabby to the touch. The erect brow was firm still, and the small black eyes brutal and active, but the skin of the cheeks and the puffed underlids had begun to pucker and to decay, and the hung leathers of the jaw-flesh drooped in folds, like an unfixed curtain, over the bones of the face and upon the baggy throat. Yet her hair was sleek and black, coiled round and round her large and orderly head in long thin plaits, glistening in the sun like jet, and she wore unmoved in the silent deluge of erect sunshine a thick black skirt and bodice and a black shawl crossed upon her breast. She began to beat with her heavy red hollystick upon the ground.

As she watched the young man mowing in her field she heard again from the kitchen the rising hysteria of her daughter's voice, imploring Christ to let it stop, beseeching Jesus to let it stop. She fidgeted, striking the glittering dust with her stick, enraged at the raucous distress of the voice and the endlessly repeated prayer that became louder and louder as she listened, she felt the tension increase like the unbearable slow opening of a furnace door, and at last she rose in anger, crying out in a loud voice as she powdered her way forward, blaming her daughter and taunting her, bearing her merciless dark flesh up towards the black door of the house with hulking stateliness. She left her stool and trampled through the dust as it were in fetters, and reaching the house began to curse the afflicted voice of her child and her endless prayers, shouting aloud and hammering with despotic fists for respite and silence upon the door.

But in spite of the blows and the menacing words the imbecile chant was repeated – 'O Jesus, let it stop, O Jesus, let it stop,' the girl screamed out, and the old woman began battering at the bolted door with the polished hollystick that shook out violent flashes like the spokes of a spun wheel; she clutched her heavy red stick with both her powerful hands, the repellent skin of her brown face lifted from her teeth like lunacy and her lip in her mouth, she struck again and again at the sounding woodwork, insane with hatred, using the maniacal energy of her joints to plaster the rowdy boards with a heavy machine-like weight of blows, trying to overwhelm the screamed gibberish of prayers.

Then suddenly the savage noise of hammering was over and in the silence the old woman leaned flushed and hunch-shouldered towards the door, she held her brooding sullen face close to the smouldering door, breathing heavily upon it, listening for her daughter's voice, her ponderous ungainly flesh relaxed as though the insane puppet-strings which jerked energy through her erect stature dangled for a moment slack upon her joints.

But the crying voice was mute and a tingling silence spread itself out over the dust of the hot slope. The old woman lowered her stick and turned, awkward as a hobbled animal, away, pushing in the dishevelled corner of her shawl and twisting the snake-like tail of a jetty plait back into the coils of her hair. She looked out frowning and panting towards the sunny field, and there the lemon-haired workman had lowered his scythe and, shading his eyes, was gazing up towards the house in puzzlement at the unhidden scandal of the shouted curses and the beaten door. Instantly she screamed at him, incoherent again with fury, waving her fiery stick and beating the ground in clownish frenzy, she laughed, her teeth set and showing, and a convulsive grimace on her swarthy face, as the young man began to slave once more at his mowing.

.   .   .   .   .

Inside the house the yellowish heat of the room was oppressive and motionless. A scalding yellow shawl drawn like a curtain across the window dimmed the air and tried to withhold the strong sunlight from the red hump of fire smouldering in the grate. Flies laboured in a ring before an indistinguishable picture hung above the tarred chimneypiece. After the uproar of the hammering upon the door the grey girl rocked herself from side to side, dim and unreal as a phantom in the shadows of a settle, babbling to herself and fretfully boring with her large fingers into the palms of her hands. She was a tall grey-clad figure, very angular and a hunchback, dressed in clothes similar to her mother's, but the shapeless and baggy garments were pale grey, the heavy skirt and the thick fringed shawl folded around her humped shoulders were of silvery greyish wool. She wore a sort of soiled handkerchief spread out on top of the plentiful and fluffy hair of her head. Her small bony face was thin and undeveloped and, apart from her eyes, large, abject and gentle, she was hideous. A sickly greyish skin moist with grease covered her watchful sharp-edged features, and a pair of taut sinews strained in unrelaxed and ugly prominence across her sunken cheeks. But, as she sat with the yellow gloom falling upon her glistening skin and her pallid clothes, she looked dim and unsubstantial, her pale face and her uncoloured fluffy hair and the nacrous bulges of her red-rimmed eyes made her appear spectral and shadowy, her figure seemed almost transparent in its greyish coverings. In the stupefying heat she no longer prayed but jabbered about the trees and the primroses and the buds.

Spring had come once, daily her uneasy heart had watched it through its bars. Morning after morning she had heard the throaty lecherous whistle of the thrush, and looking out into a raw dawn she saw the sky glow dull and red as the back of a mirror. She went down into the misty field when the vast shadows lying upon the earth were still white with hoarfrost and sat crouching in the hedge, fearing the long flock of starlings that wavered low overhead like the skin of a spotted serpent. She gazed with her

bulging whitish eyes at the small dewdrops on the faces of the
pale primroses, the minute drops of moisture like a tiny perspiration spread out upon the yellow petals, and when the curve
of birds writhed by again she hurried home fearfully, high
shouldered and with long strides. Each morning she escaped to
the field and at last the buds of the little horse-chestnut in the
hedge began to crack open upon their branches. She stood
gazing in ecstasy at the fine white velvet of the breaking buds,
the delicate grey-green birth-fur covering the infant leaves as
they unfolded from their husky glues. She stood forgetful,
watching the static gesticulation of those little grey-gloved
hands, the grey-green herringbone of the leaves standing up
crumpled from the splitting buds.

And then suddenly she heard a shout. She looked round, it
was the radiance of broad daylight and the great trees were
drying in the sun. Her heart seemed to leave her body and
return again burning like a hot spark to her breast. Up the
gritty path she ran, avoiding the demented old woman who
waited massive and wine-faced with fury at the roadside,
striking a convulsive blow at her with her red stick as she passed.
She reached the house and flinging herself with prayers into the
kitchen settle, waited in agony to see the loutish figure fill the
door.

The young man worked the slow circuit of the field, his feet
in their heavy boots crawling one after the other in the stubble,
and the scythe-blade flashing through the packed stems in an
arc of which his body was the liquid axle. There was a buttercup
growing out of his faintly-bearded mouth and his hair was short
and bright yellow, almost the colour of a clump of stone-crop,
standing up with the vigour of young wheat upon his head. He
wore the dress of a travelling labourer, a dark blue flannel shirt,
cream corduroy trousers belted at the waist and heavy hobnailed boots. His sleeves were rolled up to the shoulders baring

his large tawnied arms, and his blue shirt, open to the waist, hung in a hollow bladder from his coloured body as he crouched with solicitude and absorption over his scythe. The heat of the unsheltered field was burdensome but he continued to prowl intently through the golden-haired grass, the liquid action of his body appeared easy and graceful, he seemed easily to skid the cutting blade over the roots of the grasses, severing the crowded stalks in armfuls as he crept forward. Although he was not tall he bent over the scythe and diminished it with his skill and the grace and fluid sweetness of his stroke; he huddled his body over it protectively, and it became light and almost toylike in his hands. From the corner of the field where the grass rose to his belt he could see the old woman sitting with the rigid inactivity of a puppet outside the house, her red varnished stick across her knees and the metal toes of her clogs glistening in the sun. Then, when he was out of sight of the path, he stopped and leaned back under the young horse-chestnut tree, where the hay rope was that he wound round his scythe-blade, and his bottle and his food-basket, sheltered under his black coat from the sun.

As he chewed his bread he looked up at the scene around him, the desert hills and the mountains above, the bare squalid peaks smouldering in a dung-brown row, porous and pitted with large sponge-holes, the parched earth giving up its heat like an oven. He saw around him outside the field the stunted scrub tortured on the unslaked dust of the mountain; but down in the bottom of the valley were the trees and the fields swimming in a flood of green verdure.

There was silence now on the sun-sodden slope, and remembering the old woman's attack upon the door he looked up at the house clinging low to the side of the bare mountain at the end of the field. It was white-washed and stone-roofed, it looked dead in the glare of the afternoon, like the incrustation covering some torpid creature motionless under its shell on the barren rock. He smiled to himself, thinking of the frightened inmate, wondering at the raving hatred of the old woman. He finished his food

and pulling the petals in bunches from the purple clover blooms
he bit the sweetness out of the ends of them with his front teeth.

The girl slept with her long body stretched across the table
and her rigid arms pushed out before her. A line of spittle hung
from the corner of her twitching mouth on to the boards. She
wore over her face and over her whole body a protective mem-
brane of greyness, almost like an obscuring moss, she was
enveloped in a grey film like a natural silvery-greyish down. She
lay stiffened across the table and when at last she began to
awaken, her spirit bruised and uneasy, she lifted up her head
from the boards and her large lustrous eyes went round the walls
in anguish and bitter recognition. The tap sounded again and
she rose to her feet, her glance bounding round the room towards
the door and back again to the window. She stood restlessly
twisting together her huge fingers, feeling the little streams of
hot sweat trickling over her body and the strong blows of her
heart rocking her tall flesh upon her naked feet.
And then, trying to prevail against her terror, she began
anxiously to wade like a gawky flightless bird towards the
window, she dipped forward with excitement and apprehen-
sion, bony and deformed, her head thrust out and nodding
before her, and her bare soles whispering warily on the flags.
At the window she drew back the warm shawl, and confronting
her the other side of the glass were the wet head and wide
shoulders of the young workman, a smile upon his tanned and
tranquil face. At the sight of him, standing so close to the
window, she was startled and afraid, the dizzy walls slid round
her and went black with the heavy plodding of her heart.
Mechanically she hooked the curtain clear, and then she began
fiddling feverishly with the twisted fringes of her grey shawl. In
the fierce sunlight his dense short hair shone clear yellow,
almost lemon-coloured, and his eyebrows appeared in a pale
and fluffy line with the intense blue eyes contracted beneath

them. As he grinned out of his faint yellow beard a bubble burst over his mouth, and he showed in his sunburnt face an unbroken shelf of white teeth.

The girl felt powerless under his longlashed gaze, the bewildered flesh of her limbs was numb, heavy and fatigued. He began to perform the action of raising a bowl from the sill, and although she understood him she remained bulge-eyed and immovable, staring out in panic through the shut window at the vivid and miniature scene behind him, the thick blue sky and the moulted hills and the block of uncut grass in the middle of the field. She was conscious of the cupped hands raised to the white-smiling mouth, and the golden-crested head, beady with sweat, tilted backwards in the sun, but she could not budge to grasp the window-bolt, she felt helpless and lazy in his presence, she stood bewildered by the obstinacy of her heavy limbs. She knew she must open the window, but before his bearded smile and his mimicry her will was dried up with terror, and her indolent long arms hung down beside her as though in great weariness, loaded with ungoverned bunches of heavy fingers. And all the while, as her heavily beating heart plundered blood and her desire out of her limbs, the tranquil brown face beyond the glass continued to smile and the bewildering hands journeyed again patiently to and from the mouth.

The flesh of the girl's feet clave to the flagstones, she could not open to him, she shrank in anguish from laying her languid hands upon the blazing fabric before her, the fiery doorway of that single window-pane. Her body resisted and remained inactive with distress and bewilderment, seeing the glint of the thick golden hairs on the man's bare arms, and the smile of entreaty and gentle mockery on his wet face. She glanced round at the kitchen door and then moved in a sudden reversal of her agony, she dropped sideways as though she had been cut down and crouching beside the water-jar dipped the hanging tin cup into it. This she bore splashing to the window, and when she had drawn back the bolt, she placed the spilling tin in the waiting hands of the workman.

Outside, the white butterflies blew sparkling over the grass and a jittering blackbird scissored his startled way across the field. As the workman swallowed his drink the girl turned round and stared with the goggling eyes of a victim at the kitchen door, her huge wet eyes started out bulbous with terror from their red lids and the glazed skin of her greasy face shone. Half consciously through her panic she heard the thunderous cracking of the heated timbers above her head, and the gulping of the workman's throat as he swallowed the water out of the tin cup. In spite of her trembling body she flooded her desperate will into the room, trying with her resistance to seal up between its lintel and its threshold the bolted door through which her mother might enter the kitchen. She stood fiercely facing the wall, her face gleaming with the lustre of perspiration spread over it, and her woollen clothes grey and rough against the incandescent rod of sunlight leaning into the room, as though they were hoary with a felt of mist or minute rain. Over the skin of her back and her flanks ran the sweat in long wet lines and her body was becoming limp and exhausted, the uncontrollable blood seemed to be retreating from her knocking head and climbing up out of her bare feet.

Then suddenly she heard the workman's voice at her back thanking her for the water. Her fists opened and the thin cords pulled out across her cheeks subsided. Stepping forward through the glowing probe of sunlight, and without raising her eyes to the man's smile, she snatched back the tin and slammed the window against him. Then, when she had unhooked the curtain, the place became dim again, and in her relief she began whimpering and clapping her large frenzied hands in the four corners of the room, catching the flies. 'Jesus, Jesus,' she muttered to herself, slapping her palms together, but all the time she remembered the crack which appeared like a white head-scar across the pane when she slammed the window.

·   ·   ·   ·   ·

Everything around the workman on the dusty hillside was silent and motionless, the earth endured her senseless load of heat and brilliance. On the green and lawny floor of the *cwm* below him grew the bladdery groves, and a flat pool of corn was yellowing amongst the green fields. Leaning with his gathered things against the little horse-chestnut trunk, he remembered the black door of the cottage with its dented boards and its beads of rosin, and the heavy iron bolt on each side of it; he thought of the heavy old woman waiting outside, her full stiff body immobile like the black hulk of some stuffed and crucified scarecrow, and her hands blackish as she counted out the silver coins of his payment. And he thought too of the terrorized head of the girl looking through the window, the small pale face with the prominent tendons across the cheeks, the eyes pale as though they were staring out over a snowfall, and the huge mop of fluffy hair damp at the roots, he remembered the glitter of alarm and revulsion that spread over her greasy and tremulous features when she saw him at the window.

Then suddenly as he leaned forward in the shadow of the slim young tree he felt her move against him, and he looked up with excitement. Her branches were swaying gently above him, almost he could hear her heart beating as she swayed forward against his breast and softly withdrew herself again, lapsing to and fro with timid grace. He stepped out into the finished field and the winds dived at him. Everything had changed in shape and colour, the sun was sealed up now behind the storm-clouds and alone, striking obliquely down into the valley on his left, was the huge nail of a sunbeam. He felt the wind come in powerful cold puffs, racing past him with the speed of a hip-deep sluice, and distantly he heard the muted cackle of thunder like a flexible cane clicking across a fence. Gathering up his belongings he ran across the field and reached the road and, as he watched the disorder of the darkening sky increase, large black clouds, like the roots of an entire uptorn forest, crept nearer, spreading their soils and their dangling tendrils low over the whole sky, and from their edges shaking out their showers over the back of the hill. Large bright drops splashed heavy as spilt lead on the gritty road, and the thunder, standing nearer, blurted out its protest with increasing frequency. Changing his mind in this heavy rain he ran hot and breathless up the slope through the mud and the young wrinkled brooks forming on the hillside, his basket under his arm and the bandaged blade of his scythe clawing the air. Reaching the house again he bounced his fist impatiently upon the black door, and the bawling inside stopped. There was a brief silence, except for the distinct rain that spat like scattered lead against the warm-blooded wall, and then he heard the voice of the old woman shouting out sharply in her bitter and vindictive tones, asking who was there.

'Let me in, let me in,' the workman replied, with the rain already through his coat. A sheety squall of lightning glittered, with the swagger and impermanence of sunlight flashed on flung water, as the voice of the old woman began frantically to curse his return, but her words were drowned by the uproar of many thunders summoned muttering and yelling through the explosive doorways. The dark sky from end to end boiled with smoke the bruised slaty shade of a blue leaf, and the white rain-rods beat into the earth at a steeper angle. Although the sun had a two-hour drop before it the daylight was almost gone; the dark muslin of rain dragged in long veils over the anni-hilated floor of the valley and only the golden lightning illu-minated the dimness, flashing its stutter upon the gloomy door.

'Let me in, let me in,' the workman shouted again with impatience, ignoring the refusal of the old woman and beating with both fists on the warm woodwork. The thunder rippled and crashed above the house and he heard the daft voice of the girl yelling out in terror, saying, 'Let him in, mother, let him in. O Jesus, Jesus, Jesus—'. Then when the old woman had bawled out brutally in reply there was a sound like a blow and a tumble, and the gurgling idiocy of the girl's voice sank to a whisper in the small silence. The workman smiled standing in the unprotected doorway with the diagonal rain pouring over him as it were from a nozzle. Then, lifting up his heavy boot, he kicked hard at the flimsy plank door and with quick blows smashed the bolt out of the doorpost on the inside. The wood splintered easily and the door flew into the room with a bang, crashing into a little table that shattered itself on the flagged floor.

In the dim room the grey figure of the girl, her face buried in her hands, was just visible as she sat sobbing on the floor in the shadows of the settle. Beside her on the hearthrug stood her mother, powerful and ugly in her black baggish clothes, the flies buzzing before her brown-skinned leather-loaded face, and circling the surly and arrogant head with the ornate plaits carefully hairpinned round it. The room looked dim as underwater brickwork, it was like a tarnished and flowerless interior viewed through a gloom of coloured glass. But the yellow curtain had been torn back from the window and there the dissolving landscape poured melting down the cracked pane.

'Why do you refuse me?' the workman asked, the pale palms of his hands facing into the room. He smiled gently from the doorway, his golden hair dark with rain, and the bright finery of the water running off his jacket and the lobes of his ears and the point of his beard on to the kitchen stones.

As they stepped out of the house the storm roared its welcome, the winds passed each other, they overleapt each other yelling over the mountain. The girl and the workman ran soaking down the hill, and sheltered under the horse-chestnut tree whose bark streamed with rain as though it had waded the river. She wore her mother's clogs but she had lost her grey shawl and the cloth from her fluffy hair. She crouched hunch-shouldered beside the workman, wiping her face and her sticking lids, her heart beating in her throat like the blood of a handled bird. Her mind was ablaze with the glaring remembrance of the brandished thicket of lightning burning at the window. 'Leave us alone,' the old woman had cried to the workman in her jarring voice, 'what have we got to do with you? What have we got to do with you?'

The workman under the tree took off his soaking jacket and put it over the girl's head.

The powerful tendrils of the storm had dragged at the house, the mother's anger was elaborate and fanatical, the daughter remembered her flushed face and her lifted lip and the heaving of her stiffened and sluggish bulk.

And now the pity of the workman's hand glowed like the glass of a hot lamp on the girl's wet arm.

At the kitchen window there had been the rustle of the pouring rain, packing, above entreaty and abuse, its silks against the pane of glass. In the wet and sunburnt grip the daughter's voice was raucous with uncontrollable anguish, it was a tearing of the chained flesh to be sundered from the hug and comfort of that tyrannical maternal body. The workman's pleading tone to the mother was decent and unharassed, but she in a spurious voice thirsted for the solace of her child, she was an old woman with her weight on her stick, and she bit into the hand firmly bangled upon her wrist.

The girl screamed at the workman's blow and the sight of her mother's falling figure, she heard the thunder crash over the stone roof of the house like the waves smashed open upon the rocks. In the light of the scribbled lightning the blood spouted out of her mother's divided face in a loop of heavy drops. The girl's bulging eyes saw the brink and the depths always black, her husky voice cried upon the help and forgiveness of Jesus, her meagre body twisted up like a device.

The rain was flooding down the road in broad pure streams, the sides and foundations of the solid hills were melting together and pouring away in floods of water. Blood from her mother's body splashed her bare feet, the powerful black hulk with its foreign flabby face hooded under the metallic hair. The hill was dark, but presently there came a vivid flash, the girl and the workman saw the whole of heaven's lightning driven sprawling out of the sky, it crashed out of the darkness and landed in outspread splendour upon the little clinging house. The walls split open and the stone roof smashed like a clay pan. The girl cried out, her feverish fingers twisted in the workman's hands. 'She's dead,' she yelled. 'O Jesus, Jesus, she's dead.'

THE FOUR-LOADED MAN

The little girl sat in the cottage kitchen drawing a fire like a rose-bunch, and a wine-cup, and a shooting star. Except for the two chalk dogs on the mantelpiece she was by herself, but she wasn't frightened although the house was lonely, and the owlish snow was swimming among the tips outside the window. In the middle of the table-top lay the long black iron house-key, and she had the red-haired fire with his frosty parable for a friend.

The clipped hair was a dark vee in the groove of the little girl's neck-nape as she bent at her chalice and her flashing star. Her large bright eyes were china brown and shiny by the blown mop of fire, and at the apple-lipped corner of her mouth grew the small brown crust of a sore the round size of a daisy-centre. She wore a warm apricot dress of wool, all lily-worked on the sleeves, and in her hair she had a crimson feather.

She heard the wind go file-screeching from the beech-boughs over the shabby mountains, and she thought of her grannie saying, 'Rhys y Mynydd.' So she took in her tongue to look at the brass-handed clock throbbing on the wall. It was time to make food, but as she passed the window she saw a man coming slowly down the tips through the thick, wrapping snowflakes. She peered out over the sulk of the window daffodils, and then she forgot about the old man in the weather and the cold kettle-lid in her hand. The torn snowflakes came swarming out at the end of the valley, the first grey crayon-work of snow was already smooth over the roundness of the tips. Her grannie's garden bramble was furred like the milky tangle of a woolball, and the tufted hedge-grass in the garden bank was bear-fur rough with snow. A small robin, an eggcupful, flicked brick-breasted among the swirling flakes.

When the old man knocked, the little girl took up the key and opened the door after she had jumped. Flakes curved past her into the kitchen like three white flies as she held the door

wide open, and the cold breeze began bee-buzzing at the firm
bird's feather in her hair.

'Is your mam in?' asked the old man.

'I haven't got a mam,' answered the little girl.

She could see the stranger was a travelling glazier-man with
large squares of glass strapped like a big window on his back.
He made the little girl laugh because his bowler hat and his long
black coat were sheeted all down the front with cracked snow as
though he wore a coating of thick white-lime. He was short and
small, very old, not much taller than the little girl herself,
although he had thick clogs of snow caked under the soles of
his boots. His shrunken face was yellow, wrinkled, the skin
sagging under his eyes, and seeming to pull down the lower lids
so that they showed the blood-shot inside flesh to the little girl.
His nose was narrow and bony, a thin pink claw, sharp-hooked
like a rose-thorn, and his heavy bottom lip hung down the
bright purple-black of tracing-paper. His scarce beard grew
in a small grey tangle, brushing over his buttoned coat-collar
with the tremble of his head. When the little girl had got him
sitting in her grannie's wicker in his shaken hat and coat, his
pack outside in the garden, she noticed that his resting hands
were high-veined down the backs, like the underside of a
rhubarb leaf, only very hairy.

But the old man's small shaking face under the bowler brim
made the little girl unhappy, it had a fume of pain always
hovering over it, and she began to wonder who the visitor was.
Because he looked so sad she thought he might be Rhys y
Mynydd, the wind-man who moaned over the mountains. So
she told him to put on his glasses to look at the drawing of the
fire-coals, and the love-cup, and the swift-prowed star. He held
the paper close up under the pink hook of his nose, bending over
and shaking so much the girl thought his eyes would drop into
his glasses, and that made her laugh again.

He said nothing about the drawing, but when he looked up
he asked:

'What is that *'smotyn* in the corner of your mouth, *cariad*?'

The little girl put her tongue on her lip-sore. 'My grannie calls it a *cusan bwbach*, a goblin's kiss,' she told him. 'And now I can ask you a thing. Why do you shiver by the fire and have leaf-lines on your face, then?'

He looked up at her, shaking. One of the eyes of his little glasses was cracked across the middle.

'It is because of the four-pointed load I have to carry,' he said, spreading his fingers before the fire.

'But not now,' said the little girl, puzzled. 'Your glass pack is leaning in the garden.'

The old man parted his purple lips smiling feebly.

'I carry the four quarters of a heavier load than that,' he answered.

'Show me your load, tell me about the four quarters of your heavy load,' cried the little girl.

The old man's top lip twitched like an eyelid. He put his glasses in his pocket and wiped his wet eyes with his cocoa-coloured handkerchief.

'My first is called my poverty,' he said.

The little girl went into the pantry and brought out some bread in her frock.

'I will cut you the kissing-crust of my little milk-loaf,' she said.

'No crust will heal my second called my loneliness,' he answered.

The little girl went to the door and pulled the big key out of the lock.

'I will give you the key of my grannie's kitchen,' she said.

'No key will heal my third called my sickness,' he answered.

The little girl remembered her grannie would jump off the arm-chair to jerk a bean through her swallow and make herself well again.

'I will help you on to the wicker and catch you when you jump to the mat,' she said.

'No jump will heal my fourth, called my old age,' he answered.

The little girl thought of her grannie saying the clock brings birthdays in his hands.

'I will cut the card out of the clock-face and my fire will burn it,' she said.

A big snow-load jumped off the roof into the garden and the old man got up and slowly opened the door. It had stopped snowing and the wind had almost gone, leaving only a finger-print crumpled on half a path-pool. Everything in the garden was still and covered with smooth snow, a cherry tree like a white growing bone, and the beech boughs, where the old man's load of glass was, weighted down with their burden of whiteness, the big branches snow-snaked and each tiny twig, perhaps no wider than an eyelash, with its little load of snow. The leaning pack of glass was covered thick with a sheet of square snow, and the little girl, with the flat of her crooked fingers pressed deep through touching the cold glass, cut a big upright cross in the middle of it; she spread a dark glass cross with her wiping finger wide in the middle of the sheet of snow.

'Remember the bread, *cariad*, and the key, and the jump, and the clock face,' said the old man, and he turned slowly away out of the garden. The little girl said, 'Goodbye, Rhys y Mynydd,' feeling sad to see him going so feebly down the path. She watched him climbing like a cripple over the tips towards the milky mountains, the big black cross bold in the white square on his back.

When he was out of sight she went into the kitchen, putting her tongue like a bud into the corner of her lip. She tasted the sore had dropped off. So she lit a candle and hunted for it under the table.

AN AFTERNOON AT EWA SHAD'S

Em was my friend. He lived with my Ewa Shad and my Bopa Lloyd in a lonely row of whitewashed cottages on the side of the hill. It was a lovely sunny afternoon when I went up there carrying a brown paper parcel, and my mother had put my blue print trousers on me. These were real trousers with a button fly and a patch pocket for my handkerchief on my behind.

Em lived in the end cottage in the row. There was a pavement in front with gutters crossing it half-filled with soapy water from the colliers' bath-tubs. In front of the pavement again stretched a flat patch of rusty ground, a sort of little platform in the side of the hill, where the sagging drying-lines stood, and a chickens' *cwtch* built of tarred orange-boxes. At the back of the row, beyond the colliers' gardens, the steep tips of pit-rubbish sloped smoothly up into the sky, and it was on these tips the men who were out of work used to scratch for coal. Em's father, my Ewa Shad, had made a fence round his garden out of old pit-rope and sheets of rusty corrugated zinc, but the bottom part of the fence was formed of the two end frames of a black iron bedstead, with the bright knobs and the brasswork still shining in the sun upon them.

I went into the back garden, and there I found Em playing with his fish. He had a zinc bath, half-filled with water, sunk to the level of the ground to keep it in. He took his finger out of his nose to wave to me. It was a good garden for playing in because only about a quarter of it was set, and the earth of the rest had been trodden hard as the flags of a kitchen. There was a sycamore tree growing in the middle, and a whitewashed *dubliw* stood like a sentry-box in the far corner. Em's father was lying on his back between the lettuce-beds, his boots off and his cap over his face. He was dirty and in his working clothes, and every now and then he would take hold of his flannel shirt and start scratching his chest with his fist.

55

'It's our Mam's birthday to-day,' said Em, as I went up to him. His jersey was navy blue, with a new light blue sleeve to one arm and a new half sleeve, from the elbow down, to the other. He was sunburnt, his nose dotted with black freckles like the spots on a bird's egg, and his ginger hair was cut very short and in a notchy way, looking as though something had been nibbling at it. I could see he had a red blood-shot blot in his eye that afternoon, and I thought I would like to have one of those too. We played with the fish which was about as big as my middle finger, and which had a bright scarlet line all around the gulping edge of its mouth.

Presently Bopa Lloyd came out of the kitchen to throw some potato peelings over the fence. When she saw me she looked glad, and when I gave her the parcel for her birthday she patted my face like a pony. She was a fat woman wearing a black flannel bodice with grey pin-stripes, and a wet sack apron that hurt you when she wiped your nose with it. On her forehead she had lines across like you use for music, and her grey hair was coming down out of her combs like the feathers of an untidy hen. Her nostrils were black and big enough for her to put her thumbs up them, and there were three or four little round lumps of shiny purplish skin growing on her face, each one very smooth and tight-looking and with a high polish on it. And one of these lumps, the glossy plum-coloured one on her chin, had a long brown hair curling out of the top of it. 'Shad,' she shouted, 'come from by there now and wash yourself for dinner.'

Just then a big drop of rain fell into the middle of the pan where Em's fish was. The sycamore opened and let out a bird. Loads of dark clouds, with torn wispy edges like black heavy hay, were blown across the sky, joining up and soon leaving no blue. It became dark and cold, and big pieces of white water began falling heavily out of the sky and dropping cold as lead right through my thin blouse, wetting my skin. Bopa Lloyd hurried towards the kitchen door with her parcel like a hen off her nest, shouting to us: 'Go and shelter in the dubs while I get your dinner or you'll get wet soaking.' Em and I ran into the

W.C. and Ewa Shad got up too and trotted down the garden, the peak of his cap on his neck and his working boots under his armpits. 'I been with the angels,' he muttered as he passed us, and we sat and watched him till the kitchen door had gulped him through.

Soon it was raining like tapwater and we heard the bumming of the thunderclap, but it was a long way off. From where we were, we could see a big rain-stream pouring along a gutter the coal pickers had worn down the side of the steep tip outside the garden, and half-way down, where it met a big lump of orange shale, it spouted up into the air, curving high out like a fountain. We sat on the wooden seat of the *dubliw* watching the inky tips through the open door. Then, when Em peeped out, he said the down-pipe from the troughing next door was pouring rain into his garden. I could see it was broken off halfway down, and it swung loose against the wall like the empty coat-sleeve of a man with one arm, making a big rusty tobacco-stain on the white-lime of the wall. Em ran out into the rain, picked up the piece of downpiping that had fallen into his garden, and sloped it from the wall to the edge of his zinc bath sunk into the earth. Then he ran back again, and we waited for the pan to fill to the brim with water.

We could see the earth spitting hard with rain, and hear it hissing like poured sugar or a cockle-bed. Grey rain-fur grew round the pit-ropes of the garden fence and the iron bedstead, and over the sheets of rusty zinc. The surface of the water in the bath swarmed with tall rain, each heavy drop as it fell bouncing up again like the bobbing rod on the top of a sewing-machine. Then two of Bopa Lloyd's hens, a white one and a ginger one, struggled through the hedge into the garden, their feathers stuck to them with rain. 'Shoo,' said Em, and the white one fell into the bath. Em laughed, but the chicken made so much noise Bopa Lloyd came out to the door of the kitchen, drying her hands on her sack apron. When she saw what had happened she pushed Ewa Shad back in and, swinging a towel over her head, she ran round the side of the house and got a big shovel out of the coal-house. It was a collier's shovel, an old one of Ewa Shad's, shaped like a heart-shaped shield. With this she shovelled the chicken up out of the pan while the water ran out of the tool-bar hole in the corner. She kicked down the piping Em had sloped from the wall and shouted, 'Come on in now, boys, and have a meal of food.'

It was dark inside Bopa Lloyd's kitchen, but I could smell the fried onions and herrings cooking for dinner in the big fire-place, where the row of bright candlesticks was and the brass horses in the hearth. The ceiling was brown wood with beams across, and the stairs curved down into the far corner. Some sheets of newspaper and two pieces of sacking covered the parts of the floor you walked on. When the back door opened it banged against the mangle, which had a couch alongside with a bike on it. The wallpaper was brownish with purple birds and upright daisy chains of black roses, but Ewa Shad hadn't put it on properly near the curve in the wall made by the stairs, and all along that side the stripes were diagonal. Our Mam said Ewa Shad must have two left hands.

'Emlyn,' said Bopa Lloyd, 'go and fetch your father's slaps.'

Four of us sat down to dinner, Bopa Lloyd, Ewa Shad, Em, and myself. Ewa Shad had washed a bit now, the middle of his face and the palms of his hands. He was a funny-looking man, pale, with a big oval face and round popping eyes, whitish grey and very shiny and wet-looking. On his head he had a brown covering of my father's armpit hair, and now that he had taken off his red flannel muffler I could see the swelling wen hung in his neck like a little udder, the upper half of it grimy and the bottom half clean and white. When I went into the kitchen he was rubbing his back up and down against the edge of the open pantry door to scratch himself. He didn't say anything to me, he just rubbed and showed his teeth with the dirty dough on them. Then he sat down and read the tablecloth with his head twisted round on one side.

Bopa Lloyd sat on a chair without a back nearest the fire,

with her false teeth on the table in front of her. 'There's pretty trousers you've got on,' she said, as she served me half a herring. 'Let me see, a pocket and a coppish and all.'

Ewa Shad ate his potatoes and onions without saying a word, but he looked over all his food before he ate it, and sometimes he gave a loud wet belch. And every now and then he would start scratching himself, putting his arm inside his shirt and rubbing his chest, working around under his armpit to his back, and at last letting his fingers come back up through his open collar-band on to his wen. I was looking most of the time at the little purple potatoes sprinkled on Bopa Lloyd's face; they were so tight they looked inflamed, like little bladders ready to burst. Then I heard Ewa Shad and Bopa Lloyd talking loudly. Suddenly my Ewa stopped and stared before him with his mouth open. I could see the spittles stretched like thin wires from his top teeth to his bottom ones in an upright row.

'You'll be sorry,' he growled at Bopa Lloyd at last. 'You'll be sorry,' and he left the table and went up the stairs out of sight.

'What's the matter with him now, our Mam,' said Em, as though he was going to cry. 'What's he gone to bed without washing for?'

'Because he's gone dull,' said Bopa Lloyd, running her finger round her gums, her face very red. 'Since he's lost his job he's not a-willing to eat his fried onions if they're not all in proper rings. He's going daft, that's what's the matter with him.' Then she went quieter. 'Have you had enough of food, *bach*?' she said to me, putting her teeth back in her mouth. 'Don't take no notice of him. Try a bit of teeshun lap, will you?'

When she had sharpened the carving knife on the doorstep, Em and I sat down on the cold stone, eating our cake and playing dixstones. We could hear Ewa Shad thudding about in his stocking-feet upstairs. The rain was slackening and by the time we had reached fivesy, it had stopped.

'Can we go out now, our Mam?' said Em.

Bopa Lloyd was sitting on the couch by the bike, sewing

Ewa Shad's coat up under the armpit, and she said we could. We went into the garden. The heavy rain had made the place look different, there was gravel about, and dirty pools with small-coal in them like mushroom-gravy. And the earth smelt strong as an animal. But the sky was clearing again, although the sunshine seemed weak after the rain. Then after a bit, as Em was pulling up a long worm to give to his fish, we heard someone throwing the upstairs window open, the one with the blue blouse across for a curtain, and Bopa Lloyd, her face very red, leaned her body far out of it with her hands on the sill. 'Stay where you are,' she shouted, waving her arm, and then, clapping her hand to her teeth, she disappeared suddenly, like a sloped nail driven out of sight into a piece of wood with one blow. And then we saw a big heap of bedclothes like a large white cauliflower bulging out through the open window, with smoke oozing upwards in thin grey hairs from it, as Bopa Lloyd pushed it out; and almost as soon as she had dropped it into the garden she came running out of the kitchen door. She began dragging the smoking bundle of sheets and blankets across the wet garden towards Em's bath of water. 'The silly flamer,' she kept on saying, 'the silly flamer. Matches with blue heads again. Every time he sees those flaming things he does something dull.' She piled the smoking bedclothes into the bath and at that Em began to cry.

'What are you grizzling at?' she asked, turning her red face towards him as she stooped.

'My fish,' he answered, pulling a little Union Jack out of his pocket. 'You'll kill it, our Mam; it's in the bath.'

'Fish, *myn uffern i*,' she cried. 'Your father sets the feather bed on fire and you grunt about your fish. Get out of the road or I'll brain you.'

She stirred the bedclothes and spat on the garden. Em and I moved away and climbed over the wet bedstead. As we went slowly up the tip, Em wiping his eyes with his flag, we could see her standing in the garden striking a boxful of matches one by one, while Ewa Shad's two big staring eyes watched her without moving over the blue blouse in the bedroom window.

We wandered about on the flat top of the tips for a long time, afraid of Bopa Lloyd. Em showed me the hole where Ewa Shad had been scratching for coal. At last we came in sight of the old air-shaft in the distance, and Em said, 'Let's go right up to it.' The shaft was a pale yellow tower shaped like a light-house standing far up on the lonely side of the mountain. To get at it we had to go through a lot of brambles and tall bracken with snakes in it, but we didn't get very wet because we kept to the path. There had been a lean rainbow, but as we went towards the tower the sun blazed again, and the tips steamed like a train in a cutting. The tower was very tall and built out of some cracking yellowish brick like shortbread. Some of the bricks were missing here and there, and right down, level with the ground, we found a good-sized hole in the side. Em put his notchy head in and said, '*Brain*, look down there.'

I lay down beside him on the steaming stones and looked into the dim hole. Every small sound resounded there, it was like putting your head into the hollow between the two skins of a drum. The shaft inside was huge, like a vast empty hall, like some shabby ruin with the floor gone through, very cold and bleak, the walls disappearing below us into the blackness, making you feel giddy and sick. And the spiders hung their webs there, round like a gramophone record, or strong and dusty as sacking. Then Em picked up a piece of brick and pitched it into the darkness. It plunged down out of sight like a diving bird and we could hear it striking the sides of the shaft from time to time with a note like the loud pong of a pitchfork, and a stone howling over the ice. Then, when we had waited and waited, staring down with our heads hanging over the cold blackness, we heard a terrible splash and roar, like a train in a tunnel, as the stone at last exploded on the water at the bottom of the shaft. The hollow pit broke out at once into an uproar, it was filled with a storm of echoes and the splashing noises of the water, and when at last all the sounds had died away the darkness was as still and silent as before. I felt sick and frightened, and we ran away together, a long loose patch across the behind of Em's trousers flapping like a letter-box in the breeze.

At last we reached the garden again and climbed the warm bedstead, and Em made straight for the bath to look for his fish. 'Go and ask Mam for a jam-jar,' he said to me, 'she'll give it to you.'

I went up to the kitchen door and opened it. It was dim inside at first, but I could see Ewa Shad sitting on the bottom step of the stairs that curved down into the kitchen. He had his shirt and trousers on, but although he was wearing his cap he had no boots on his stockinged feet. And his waistcoat was open, the front of it like a looking-glass with grease. He was catching hold of the long curved knife, the carving knife Bopa Lloyd had cut our cake with, and he was sticking the point of it as hard as he could into the side of his neck. He was using both his hands to push the knife in, and it was going through the skin just below his ear. When I saw him cutting himself like that I went cold between my legs. Every time he stabbed he jerked his head sideways to meet the knife-blade, keeping his head stiff, so that the baggy wen on the other side gave a little shiver each time the point of the knife went out of sight into the side of his neck. There was blood all round his chin and his throat and down the front of his shirt, red and thick like jam. When I had watched him give two or three slow hard stabs like this, showing his teeth out of the froth round his lips, he stopped and stared at me with his swollen white eyes. Then he pulled up the leg of his trousers and started to scratch the back of his calf as hard as he could.

His scratching seemed to go on a long time and then, just as he was about to start using the knife again, Em screamed at my side and Bopa Lloyd came down the stairs, her nostril-holes like thimbles as I looked up into them. When she saw what was happening, she pushed down the steps past Ewa Shad, snatched the knife from his hand and threw it on the fire. His eyes were like big, white, milk-bubbles staring up at her, and the lining was showing at the back of his cap. Gradually he slipped sideways on his step as though he was going to fall to the ground.

Then with a shout Bopa Lloyd pushed Em and me out into the yard, turning the key in the lock behind us.

Em stood crying by the kitchen door, rattling the clothes-peg latch, and sometimes going to the window to look in over the cardboard mending the bottom panes. In a few minutes Bopa Lloyd unlocked the door and peeped out, and I had a whiff of the handle of the knife smouldering in the grate. Her red face glowed, it was the colour of a low fire, and the grey feathers of her hair were nearly all out of her combs. 'Go home now, there's a good boy,' she said to me, 'and tell your mother, thank you for the parcel and will she come up as soon as she can.'

'What's the matter with our Dad?' asked Em, making a face and crying all over his mouth.

'He's better now,' she answered. 'Go and play with your fish, there's a good boy.'

As I went home down the road I could see the blood-shot mark like a little smudge of red-ink on Em's eye, and I thought again how lucky he was to have that. I told my mother how Bopa Lloyd's chicken had fallen into the bath, and how Ewa Shad had stuck a knife in his neck and made it bleed. And every time I went into the pantry in the dark, or when I closed my eyes, I could see the inside of the air-shaft with the big drop below me, and that made me feel sick and giddy. As my mother was dressing to go up to Ewa Shad's, she said, 'The fool couldn't even cut his throat tidy.'

WAT PANTATHRO

I got the crockery and the bloater out of the cupboard for my father before going to bed. He would often cook a fish when he came in at night, using the kitchen poker to balance it on because we didn't have a gridiron. Then I lit my candle in the tin stick, and when I had blown out the oil-lamp I went up-stairs to bed. My father was a horse-trainer, and on the hand-rail at the top of the stairs he kept three riding saddles, one of them very old, with leather handles in front curved upwards like the horns of a cow. We slept in the same bedroom, which was low and large, containing a big bed made of black iron tubes with brass knobs on the corner posts. Behind our thin plank door we had a cow's-horn coat-hook on which hung a trainer's bridle, one with a massive bit and a heavy cluster of metal fingers like a bunch of keys, to daunt the young horses. There were no pictures or ornaments in our bedroom, only a green glass walking-stick over the fireplace, and my father's gun-licence pinned into the bladdery wallpaper. When I had un-dressed I said my prayers against the patchwork quilt which my mother had finished the winter she died. Then I climbed up into the high bed and blew the candle out.

But I couldn't sleep at first, thinking of my father taking me down to the autumn horse fair the next day. I lay awake in the rough blankets hearing the squeak of a nightbird, and Flower uneasy in her stall, and the hollow dribble of the dry plaster trickling down behind the wallpaper on to the wooden floor of the bedroom. I dozed, and when I awoke in the pitch darkness I could see narrow slits of light, like scattered straws, shining up through the floorboards from the oil-lamp in the kitchen beneath me, and by that I knew my father was home. And soon I was glad to see the light go out and to hear him groping his way up the bare stairs, muttering his prayers to himself and at last lifting the latch of our bedroom door. I didn't want him to think he had wakened me because that would worry him, so I pretended to be asleep. He came in softly, lit the candle at the bedside and then finished the undressing and praying he had started on his way upstairs.

My father was very tall and slender, his hard bony body was straight and pole-like. At home he always wore a long check riding-jacket, fawn breeches and buttoned corduroy gaiters. He had an upright rubber collar which he used to wash with his red pocket-handkerchief under the pump, but because he had not been to town there was no necktie round it. His face was long and bony, dull red, or rather purplish all over, the same colour as the underside of your tongue, and covered with a mass of tiny little wormy veins. He had thick grey hair and rich brown eyebrows that were curved upwards and as bushy as a pair of hairy caterpillars. And when he pushed back his brick-coloured lips, baring his gums to get rid of the bits of food, his long brown teeth with the wide spaces between them showed in his mouth like a row of flat and upright bars.

He stood beside the bed for a moment, wiping the greasy marks off his face with his scarlet handkerchief. He did this because when he balanced his fish over the fire it often tumbled off into the flames and became, by the time it was cooked, as black and burnt as a cinder. Then, when he had done, he blessed me with tobacco-smelling hands and laid down his warm body with care in the bed beside me. I listened, but I knew he had not been drinking because I could not smell him, or hear the argument of the beer rolling round in his belly.

The next morning we went down to the fair in the spring body. This was a high black bouncy trap running on two very tall thin wheels that were painted a glittering daffodil yellow. It had a seat with a back to it across the middle and a tiger rug for our knees. Flower, my father's beautiful black riding mare, was between the shafts in her new brown harness, her glossy coat shining in the sun with grooming until she looked as though she had been polished all over with hair-oil. As I sat high above her in the springy cart I could see her carrying her small head in its brown bridle a little on one side as she trotted sweetly along. I loved her, she was quiet and pretty, and I could manage her, but I was afraid my father would sell her in the fair and buy a younger horse for training.

The hedges that morning were full of birds and berries. The autumn sun was strong after the rain and the long tree shadows in the bright fields were so dark that the grass under them seemed burnt black with fire. The wheels of the light cart gritted loudly on the road and the steel tyre came turning up under my elbow, as it rested on the narrow leather mudguard. We sat with the tiger-skin rug over our knees, my father beside me holding the brown reins loosely and resting the whip across them, the palms of his hands yellow with nicotine almost to his wrists. He looked fresh and handsome in the bright morning, wearing his new black riding-coat and his best whipcord breeches, and his soft black hat with the little blue jay's feather in it tilted on the side of his head. And round his upright collar he had a thick scarlet scarf-tie smelling of camphor, with small white horse-shoes sprinkled all over it.

I said to him, 'We are not going to sell Flower are we, my father?'

'No, little one,' he answered, teasing me, 'not unless we get a bargain, a biter or a kicker, something light in the behind that no one can manage.' And then, with his tusky grin on his face, he asked me to take the reins while he struck a match on the palm of his hand and lit another cigarette.

It was six miles down to town and all the way my father waved his whip to people or drew rein to talk to them. Harri Parcglas, taking his snow-white nanny for a walk on the end of a thirty-foot chain, stopped to ask my father a cure for the warts spreading on the belly of his entire; the vicar under his black sunshade put his hand, from which two fingers were missing, on Flower's new collar of plaited straw and reminded my father he was due to toll the funeral bell the next day; and

Lewsin Penylan the poacher, coming from his shed, brought a ferret whose mouth he had sewn up out of his inside pocket, and offered us a rabbit that night if my father would throw him a coin for the shot. It was on the hill outside Lewsin's shed a month or two ago that I had been sheltering from the pelting storm after school when I had seen my father, soaking wet from head to foot, passing on his way home to Pantathro. He was riding a brisk little bay pony up from town, his long legs hanging straight down and nearly touching the road. He had no overcoat on and the heavy summer rain was sheeting over him from the cloudburst, and running off his clothes as though from little spouts and gutters on to the streaming road. But although he was drenched to the skin, and there wasn't a dry hair on the little brown pony, he was singing a hymn about the blood of Jesus Christ loudly to himself as the rain deluged over him. When he saw me he didn't stop the pony, he only grinned, and shouted that it looked devilish like a shower. The boys who were with me laughed and pointed at him, and I blushed with shame because they knew he was drunk again.

We came down into the town at a sharp trot and I could see the long narrow street before us crowded with people and animals. There were horses of every size and colour packed there, most of them unharnessed and with oil shining in the sun on their black hoofs, and yellow, red and blue braids plaited into their manes and tails. And there was a lot of noise there too, men shouting and horses neighing and clattering about. The horses were all over the roads of the town, and over the pavements as well, standing about in bunches or being led by rope halters up and down the street, or disappearing through the front doors of the public-houses behind their masters. I hardly ever came to town and I loved it. From the high position in the cart where we sat, the crowd of bare backs before us seemed packed together as close as cobblestones, so that I thought we should never be able to get through. But my father governed our mare with his clever hands. He kept her going, waving his whip gaily to people he knew, even sometimes urging her into a little trot, easily steering his zigzag way among the mixed crowds of men and horses around us. And as we passed along he had often to shout, 'No', with a grin on his face, to a dealer who asked him if Flower was for sale or called out naming a price for her. Because our mare was pretty and as black as jet and many people wanted her.

But just when we were taking the sharp turn out of Heol Wen at the White Hart corner, breaking into a trot again, suddenly, without any warning, we came upon Tal y Fedw's big grey mare, a hulking hairy cart-horse standing out at right angles from the pavement, with her thick hind legs well forward into the narrow street. Without hesitating for a moment, my father leaned over and took the turn, and the axle-hub struck the big mare a stinger across her massive haunches as we passed, sending her bounding forward and then in a twist up into the air on her hind legs with pain and fright. The Tal y Fedw brothers, two short black little men, ran out at once cursing and swearing into the road to get hold of her head, which she had torn loose from them. I was shocked and excited and I clung to the mudguard, because the light trap, with all the leathers wheezing, rocked over on its springs as though it was going to capsize with the suddennesss of the blow. And Flower, frightened by the shouting and by the unexpected shudder of the cart behind her, threw back her head and tried to swerve away across the road. I looked up anxiously at my father. He was grinning happily, showing the big boards of his teeth in his reddish face. He didn't stop at all when Tal y Fedw swore and shouted at him, he only whipped the mare up instead.

My father sold Flower after all to a man he met in the bar of the Three Horseshoes, the inn where we put up. Then, after the business was over, we went across to the large flat field which the farmers used for the horse fair. We wandered about for a time talking to many people and listening to the jokes of

the auctioneers, but I was down-hearted because I wouldn't
see Flower any more. And in the end my father bought a lovely
slender mare, with a pale golden coat to her shining like the
wing-gloss of a bird, and a thick flaky cream-coloured tail
reaching almost to the grass. She was shod but she seemed wild,
only half-broken, with wide-open black nostrils, and a thick-
haired creamy mane, and large dark eyes curving and shining
like the balls of black marble on a gravestone. In a nearby field
a fun fair was opening, and each time the loud roundabout
siren hooted the tall filly started as though she had received a
slash with a cutting whip, her large black nostrils opened wide
with fear at the sound, and she began dancing up her long
slender forelegs off the grass as though a current of terror were
shooting through her fetlocks. She edged warily out of my
father's reach too, as long as she could, keeping at the far end
of the halter-rope, and when he put out his hand towards her
dark muzzle she shied away in a panic, peeling open the terrified whites of her eyes as they stood out black and solid from
her golden head. But he wouldn't have that from any horse and
after a time she became quiet and docile, fawning upon him,
and allowing him to smooth, with hands that were almost the
same colour, the glossy amber of her flanks. Then, telling me to
fetch her over to the 'Shoes, he handed me the halter-rope and
walked off laughing with the man who had owned her before.

It was hot and sunny in the open field then, so bright that if
a man threw up his hand it glowed crimson like a burning
torch in the sunlight. The great golden mare trod heavily
behind me, a thick fore-lock of creamy mane hanging tangled
over her eyes, and her frightened ears pricked up sharply on her
high head like rigid moon-points. I didn't want to lead her,
perhaps she was an animal nobody could manage, but I was
ashamed to show my father I was afraid. I was almost in a
panic going in the heat among the tall and awkward horses
that crowded in the field, I was afraid of being trampled down,
or of having a kick in the face from the hoof of a frightened
horse. And most of all I dreaded that the fair-ground hooter

would begin its howling again, and scare this wild creature up on to her hind legs once more with terror and surprise. It became more and more frightening, leading her across the crowded field with the hot-blast of her breath upon my flesh, I was sweating and in agony, expecting her to shy at any moment, or to rear without warning and begin a sudden stampede among the horses that crowded around us. My panic and helplessness as the tall blonde mare came marching behind me, large and ominous and with heavy breath, were like the remembered terror rippling hotly over my flesh one night as I sat alone in our kitchen through the thunderstorm, waiting for the endless tension of the dark to break.

But all the time my father, using long and eager strides, went ahead with the other man, waving his cigarette about, enjoying himself among the crowds and slapping the horses recklessly across the haunches with his yellow hand if they were in his way. 'Indeed to God, Dafydd,' he shouted, jeering at a sallow man with a fresh black eye, 'you're getting handsomer every day.'

At last the gate came in sight, my hopes began to rise that I should get out of the field before the siren blared into the sky again. To leave the fair-ground we had to cross a shallow ditch, which had a little stream in it because of the rain, and over which someone had dropped a disused oaken house-door to act as a footbridge. As soon as the young mare heard her front hoofs resounding on the wood panels she recoiled powerfully with fright and flung herself back against the rope, she began plunging and shying away from the ditch with great violence, her nostrils huge in her rigid head with surprise and terror, and the fiery metals of her shining hoofs flashing their menace in the sun above my upturned face. I was taken unawares, but I didn't think of letting go. The halter-rope became rigid as a bar of iron in my hands, but in spite of the dismay I felt at her maddened plunging, and the sight of her lathered mouth, I didn't give in to her. I clutched hard with both hands at the rod-like rope, using all my weight against her as she jerked and tugged back wildly from the terror of the ditch, her flashing forefeet pawing the air and her butter-coloured belly swelling huge above me. My father, hearing the noise and seeing the furious startled way she was still bucking and rearing on the halter-rope, ran back shouting across the wooden door, and quickly managed to soothe her again.

Meanwhile I stood ashamed and frightened on the edge of the ditch. I was trembling and I knew by the chill of my flesh that my face was as white as the sun on a post. But although I was so shaken, almost in tears with shame and humiliation at failing to bring the mare in by myself, my father only laughed, he made nothing of it. He put his hand down in his breeches pocket and promised me sixpence to spend in the shows after dinner. But I didn't want to go to the shows, I wanted to stay with my father all the afternoon.

After the meal I had the money I had been promised and I spent the afternoon by myself wandering about in the fair-ground, eating peppermints and ginger snaps. I was unhappy because my father had been getting noisier during dinner, and when I asked him if I could go with him for the afternoon he said, 'No, don't wait for me, I've got to let my tailboard down first.' I was ashamed, I felt miserable because he never spoke to me that way or told me a falsehood. In the fair-field the farm servants were beginning to come in, trying the hooplas and the shooting standings and squirting water over the maids from their ladies' teasers. I stood about watching them, and when it was tea-time I went back to the inn to meet my father as we had arranged.

My heart sank with foreboding when they told me he wasn't there. At first I waited in the Commercial, hungry and home-sick, pretending to read the cattle-cake calendar, and then I went out and searched the darkening streets and the muddy fair-ground, heavy-hearted and almost in tears, but I couldn't find him anywhere. And after hours of searching and wandering I heard with dismay a tune spreading its notes above the buildings, and I saw it was ten by the moon-faced market clock. The public-houses were emptying, so that the badly-lighted town was becoming packed with people, the fair-night streets were filled with uproar, and drunken men were lurching past, being sick and quarrelling loudly. I stood aside from them near the fishes of the monumental lamp, weary with loneliness and hunger, glimpsing through my tears the ugly faces of the men who crowded swearing and singing through the green gaslight, wondering what I should do. And then, suddenly, I realized I could hear someone singing a hymn aloud in the distance, above the noise of the town. I knew it was my father, and all my fears dropped from me like a heavy load as I hurried away, because at last I had found him.

I ran along the dark and crowded street until I came to the open square outside the market entrance, where the two lamps on the gate pillars had IN painted on them, and there I saw a swarm of people gathering into a thick circle. I failed to get through the crowd of men, so I climbed on to the bars on the market wall at the back, where the children had chalked words, and looked over the bowlers and the cloth caps of the people. There was my father, his black hat sitting on the back of his head, standing upright beneath the bright gas-lamps in an open space in the middle of the crowd, singing 'Gwaed y Groes' loudly and beautifully, and conducting himself with his two outspread arms. But although he was singing so well, all the people were laughing and making fun of him. They stood around in their best clothes, or with axle-grease on their boots, laughing and pointing, and telling one another that Pantathro had had a bellyful again. By the clear green light of the pillar globes above the gates I could see that my father had fallen, because his breeches and his black riding-coat were soiled with street dirt and horse-dung, and when he turned his head round, a large raw graze was to be seen bleeding on his cheekbone. I felt myself hot with love and thankfulness when I saw him, my throat seemed as though it were tightly barred up, but I couldn't cry any more.

He soon finished his hymn and the people began cheering and laughing as he bowed and wiped the sweat off his glistening head with his red handkerchief. And soon the serving men were shouting, 'Come on Wat, the "Loss of the Gwladys", Watcyn,' but I could see now they only wanted to make fun of him while he was saying that sad poem. I couldn't understand them, because my father was so clever, a better actor and reciter than any of them. He cleared away one or two dogs from the open space with his hat, and held up his arms for silence until all the shouting had died down; he stood dark and upright in the centre of the circle, taller than anyone around him, his double shadow thrown on the cobbles by the market lamps pointing out towards the ring of people like the black hands of a large clock. Then he spat on the road and started slowly in his rich voice to recite one of the long poems he used to make up, while I muttered the verses from the wall to help his memory.

As he recited in his chanting way he acted as well, gliding gracefully to and fro in the bright light of the ring to describe the pretty schooner shooting over the water. Or he held his tall, polelike body rigid and erect, until something came sailing at him over the mocking crowd, a paper bag or a handful of orange peel, and at that he cursed the people and threatened not to go on. When I saw them do that I went hot with shame and anger, because my father was doing his best for them. Then suddenly he stood bent in a tense position, shading his eyes, still as a fastened image with a peg under its foot, his eyes glittering under their thick brows, and the big bars of his teeth making the gape of his mouth like a cage as he stared through the storm at the rocks ahead. Rousing himself he shouted an order they use at sea, mimicking a captain, and began steering the schooner this way and that among the dangerous crags, pointing his brown finger to the thunderous heavens, burying his face in his hands, embracing himself and wiping away his tears with his coat sleeve. Every time he did something dramatic like this, although he imitated it so well that I could see the mothers kissing the little children for the last time, all the people listening laughed and made fun of him. I didn't know why they couldn't leave him alone, they were not giving him fair play, shouting out and jeering all the time at his good acting.

When the ship struck in the imitated howling of the wind he shrieked in a way that made my blood run cold, and began chasing about the open space with his arms outspread, and a frightening look of terror and despair on his face. He was acting better than ever he had done for me in our kitchen, the sweat was pouring from him now because he was doing all the parts, and yet the people were still mocking at him. Sinking his head resignedly into his hands, and dropping on one knee in the middle of the circle, he sang a few bars of the pitiful death hymn 'Daeth yr awr im' ddianc adre', in his beautiful bass voice. It was so sweet and sad I was almost breaking my heart to hear him. Some of the farm-boys took up the tune, but he stopped them with an angry wave of his hand, which made them laugh again.

And then, suddenly, he gave up singing, and as the sinking decks of the ship slid under the water, and the mothers and the little children began drowning in the tempest, he crouched down low on the cobbles with his hands clenched in agony before him, asking, with the sweat boiling out of his face, that the great eternal hand should be under him, and under us all, now and for ever. He forgot he was a drunken actor reciting before a jeering ring of people, he ignored the laughs of the crowd and behaved like a man drowning in the deep waters. He wept and prayed aloud to the King of Heaven for forgiveness, sobbing out his words of love and repentance, and when the ship with her little flags disappeared under the waves, he dropped forward and rolled helplessly over with a stunning sound, his face flat downwards on the cobbled road and his limp arms outspread in exhaustion and despair.

Just then, as he sprawled still and insensible on the cobbles like a flimsy scarecrow the wind had blown over, one of the spaniels ran up again with his tail wagging, and lifted his leg against the black hat which had fallen off and lay on the road beside my father's head. The crowd laughed and cheered more than ever when they saw that, and I could feel the scalding tears trickling down my face. I jumped down from the market wall and started to hurry the six miles home with angry sobs burning my throat, because the people had laughed at my father's poem and made him a gazing-stock and the fool of the fair.

All the afternoon I had dreaded this, and in the dark street before finding my father I had wept with alarm and fore-boding at the thought of it. I knew I should never be able to manage the golden mare alone and bring her in the night all the way up to Pantathro. And now I was doing it, holding the whip across the reins like my father, and the tall indignant creature with her high-arched neck was before me in the shafts, walking along as quietly as our Flower, and obeying the rein as though my father himself were driving her. I had prayed for help to God, who always smelt of tobacco when I knelt to him, and I was comforted with strength and happiness and a quiet horse.

The men at the Three Horseshoes who had altered the brown harness for the mare said, when I went back, that if I was Wat Pantathro's son I ought to be able to drive anything. I had felt happy at that, and ever since I had been warm and full of light inside as though someone had hung a lantern in the middle of my belly. At first I wished for the heavy bridle from the horn hanger behind our bedroom door for the mare's head, but now I didn't care, I felt sure I could manage her and bring her home alone. There was no one else on the road, it was too late, and no dogs would bark or guns go off to frighten her. And beside, it was uphill nearly all the way. Only, about a hundred yards from the railway I pulled up to listen if there was a train on the line, because I didn't want to be on the bridge when the engine was going under, but there was not a sound spreading anywhere in the silent night.

And what made me all the happier was that my father was with me, he was lying fast asleep under the tiger rug on the floorboards of the spring body. His pretty horseshoe tie was like a gunrag, and the blue jay's feather was hanging torn from his wet hat beside me on the seat, but he was safe and sleeping soundly. When the men at the 'Shoes lifted him, still unconscious, into the spring body they examined him first, holding his head up near the light of the cart lamp. I saw then that the whole side of his face was like beef, and when they pushed back his eyelids with their thumbs the whites showed thick and yellow as though they were covered with matter. And on the inside of his best breeches, too, there was a dark stain where he had wet himself; but I didn't care about that, I was driving him home myself with the young mare between the shafts and I was safe on the hill outside Lewsin Penylan's already.

The night was warm, the moon up behind me and the stars burning in front bright and clear, like little flames with their wicks newly trimmed. And in the quietness of the country the yellow trap-wheels made a pleasant gritty noise on the lonely road, and from time to time the mare struck out bright red sparks with her hoofs. We passed the vicarage where one light was still lit, and came to Parcglas, where Harri's snow-white nanny pegged on her chain chuckled at us like a seagull from the bank. I thought the mare would be frightened at this, so I spoke soothingly to her to distract her attention. She just pointed her sharp ears round and then went on, smoothly nodding her high-crested head, her golden toffee-coloured haunches working in the light of the candle flame thrown from the two cart-lamps stuck in the front of the spring body.

The sloping hedges slipped by me on both sides of the white road. I wanted more than anything else to please my father after what they had done to him, shouting he had dirtied on the swingle-tree again, and was as helpless as a load of peas; I wanted to bring him home safely by myself with the golden mare, and I knew now I should do it. Because at last I saw a star shining over our valley, a keyholeful of light, telling me I was home, and I turned into the drive of Pantathro without touching the gateposts with the hubs on either side.

THE LAST WILL

'Six golden sovereigns, and that's another hundred,' muttered my little grandfather, his face red in the great blush of sunset.

That year was so dry our water-cask split, and the rusty pump only gurgled gug-gug-gug when you worked the handle. And it was so hot your flannin shirt made you feel as though something terrible was going to happen. Then one week-night our preacher called a special meeting to pray for rain, and when my grandfather didn't trot back to his coffin after food, I thought he was going to chapel for once. I watched him lathered and in his grey-stockinged feet before the kitchen mirror – a gin advertisement it was, hanging in the open doorway – scowling like a fat-nosed Jew and scraping the growth of three days off his jowl with a cut-throat. 'Don't forget the little book, Mari *fach*, don't forget the little book,' he muttered out of a round hole in the end of his mouth to my grandmother, who was getting his black coat and waistcoat out of the mothballs, and the rubber collar with the breast attached that he wore for his funerals. When he mentioned the exercise book I knew he was going to do another will.

My grandfather was the parish carpenter and undertaker. He was a very swarthy man, squat and stout, small in the head and feet but fat around the belly, where the bulk of his weight bulged his trousers out like a giant poultice. He had only his grey flannel shirt and his baggy black ribbed trousers on now, but when he crossed the road to our zinc shed to work at the coffins, he always wore a coat braided with red piping, and a velvet smoking cap with blue forget-me-nots worked round the edge of it. I liked to see him push his cap off to scratch his scalp because the top of his tiny head was as flat as a board, and from the back he looked as though two or three slices had been cut off the top of him. But this round platform wasn't bald or smooth, it was planted with tufts of thick rough hair like little trees and shrubs, it was like a little garden with plants and bushes growing out of the top of his head. As he stood there wiping the soap from his hairy ears in the doorway, and watching the sun glowing like a big red egg in the crimson sky, he was a bit Jewish-looking, with black eyes and a big baggy nose that used to bladder out when he blew it, and a soft bristly pouch of fat sagging between his chin and the neckband of his flannel shirt. He often used to laugh when he thought of his money, opening his big black mouth, and although his gums seemed vacant, the three or four teeth that remained there were fine upstanding ivories, a bit yellowish and slimy-looking perhaps, but still gaunt and majestic in their loneliness.

But my grandfather wasn't only a carpenter and undertaker, he was a lawyer as well. If you handed a book to him, he would lower one black lid and squint along the edges of it with his carpenter's eye, because that was the only way he knew of finding out if it was a good one or not. But for all that he could read like a parson. And because he could write as well he used to draw up wills for the farmers around us who had plenty of means, and who were anxious to save a few pounds lawyer's fee that way. Usually he took me with him, and when the neighbours wanted to know how much he was asking for his trouble he would refuse anything for himself, and with a hand dark as a chimney brick on my hair, answer, 'Two pounds for the little boy,' or ,'Ten pounds for the grandson,' according to the amount of money the people had. And whatever he said they had to pay because they were afraid he would hand them the dirty end of the stick with a shabby coffin or a dear funeral.

'Come to chapel for once to-night, Dafydd Penry,' pleaded my religious grandmother as we went out of the house in our best clothes.

'Not to-night, Mari *fach*,' he answered 'not to-night. Six little pounds and we've got another hundred salted away.'

'Beware of covetousness,' she shouted after us as we went down the road, but my grandfather, who was wicked, only grinned, showing a single round white tooth like an ivory peg plugged into his upper gum.

Soon the meaty sunset was over and as we crossed the quiet fields it began to get dark. 'Whose will are you going to make, Dadcu?' I asked, going *lincyn loncyn* beside him.

'William Nantygors' at last,' he answered. 'And six of his sovereigns on to our ninety-four will make us another hundred.'

I was disappointed, it put pounds on my heart when he said where we were going, because William was a savage old creature, a widowerman everybody was afraid of, one who was always shouting out, 'Hook it, hook it,' if you went near the fences of his fields. 'They say he's a miser, Dadcu,' I said.

'He is so mean that if he had two watches he wouldn't tell you the time by one of them,' he answered.

Although I was only nine or ten, my grandfather and I were about the same height, except for his high bowler-hat. He always walked with little prancing steps, gliding up and down with his knees sagging in the way we used to play at trotting like a show pony. As he bobbed alongside me with his camphor smell, I watched the slow loll of his belly, and listened to his ripe corduroys rubbing together, wheep-wheep-wheep, at every step. Because although he had his bowler-hat on and his best coat and waistcoat, he hadn't changed his working trousers or his hobnailed boots. He said he never would any more after Didi Gai's burial, where the sexton cut the grave too narrow and he spoilt his funeral trousers digging it big enough to get the coffin in.

'Six sovereigns for another hundred,' he muttered again, lifting up his bowler and scratching among the little herbs of his head.

As we were coming down the field on the steep breast we could see Nantygors where William lived alone below us, a dirty ruin of a house with one yellow window lighted up in the pine end, and a big claw of ivy going up one side and over the roof like a birthmark growing on the side of a head. Although it was almost dark now we could make out the bog all round, the marshland that had crept closer and closer to the farm as all

William's sons had quarrelled with him one by one and left the nest for good and all.

'Nantygors,' said my grandfather, grinning and gliding, 'where we will soon be finishing another hundred, Joseph *bach*.' He trotted on, using the little tripping steps that years ago had caused the quarrel between him and William Nantygors. William, once, when he was sick in bed, had asked my grandfather to pace out the distance round his rickyard for him, so that he could buy some of the galvanized wire for it my grandfather was selling cheap. My grandfather did it and William bought the number of yards my grandfather said, but when he went to fix it, it wouldn't come to answer, he found he had about twice as much as he wanted because of my grandfather's short legs and little steps. They had words about their bargain and there hadn't been much Welsh between them for many years after that.

But before we got to the house we met Phylip Mawr Wernddu crossing the stile on his way to chapel. 'Good night children,' he said to us in the dusk, but when he saw who we were he cried, 'Hallo, Dafydd, you are going the wrong way. Supplication service to-night.'

'No, no,' answered my grandfather, still bobbing up and down but not moving forward, 'I am going to visit the sick.'

Everybody respected Phylip Mawr, he was a big heavy old man dressed all in black, with a smell of red soap and a beard like a pointing trowel. And now, because he was going to pray for rain, he had his umbrella under his arm. But my grandfather didn't like him at all because he was always asking him to come to chapel and to put his shoulder under the ark. And once he knocked at the door of our shed, where my grandfather had our heights, my own and my grandmother's, pencilled up on the wall so that he could build our coffins for us if we happened to die away from home. When my grandfather opened the door old Phylip began talking about money, stroking his beard and saying he knew where plenty of it was to be found. 'Oh, where is it to be found, Phylip *bach*,' pleaded my grandfather in great excitement, reaching for his cap and his red-piped jacket, and nearly cutting his hand in two with the chisel. 'Where is it to be found in plenty, as you say?' – 'It's a pity you don't come to chapel oftener, Dafydd Penry, and then you'd know,' said Phylip, moving off. 'On the banks of the Jordan, man, everyone must leave his riches there!'

My grandfather never liked him after that, but he had to say he was going to visit William Nantygors, who was in a very bad condition.

'Indeed,' said old Phylip, 'he is a skeleton, that's all he is, a skeleton. If you want to make his will, Dafydd Penry, you had better hurry, because he will close his eyes at any time now, poor dab.'

'I didn't say anything about making his will,' answered my grandfather, offended, dancing up and down like a cock in the snow. 'And if I am going there to do it, you remember, Phylip Thomas, I am not like the men with the quills – I never take a ha'penny for my trouble.'

'Of course you don't, Dafydd *bach*,' said old Phylip, patting me on the head, 'of course you don't. But still, the chick picks where the cock scratches. Good night, Joseph *bach*,' he said to me. 'Good night, Dafydd,' and off he went up the field to chapel, with his umbrella under his arm.

I was frightened to death, I could feel my mop standing up like knapweed on my scalp. I was sure that behind that yellow window pane I was going to see a real bone skeleton propped up white and chalky out of the bedclothes, with a skull like a large eggshell, and bare horse-teeth, and empty eye sockets, and no flesh on its bones to stop them rattling together when it moved about. I wasn't usually frightened by things like that, I was used to them. When my grandfather was busy in a hard winter, with his shed full of timber, he would often varnish the coffins on the chairs in our kitchen, and at night, if I came downstairs for a tin of water, I would pass amongst them in the firelight, just as though they were pieces of furniture. And one night Rhoda Tyllwyd, who lived two miles up the road, carried the corpse of her dead baby to our house in her shawl, almost before it was cold, to have it measured for a coffin. I saw the little bare body lying pink under the lamplight on our kitchen table, with Rhoda's big glassy tears on it like rain on cabbage, and as I helped my grandfather to run his inch-tape over it I thought nothing of it. But the picture of the old miser turned into a skeleton in that lonely house frightened the life out of me. I clung close to my grandfather in the darkness, frightened by William's washing spread out on the bushes, and nearly jumping out of my skin when his old white cow breathed hard in the dark hedge as we passed her. I would have given anything if my grandfather had said he would go back to chapel with old Phylip Mawr Wernddu.

But soon we were outside the back-door of the farmhouse. 'Only six more pounds and I'll be lying on the little feathers,' I heard my grandfather mumbling against the brickwork as he rattled the latch. In a minute or two we saw the door opening and a woman's voice said, 'Who's there?' out of the darkness of the house.

'It's me, Dafydd Penry,' answered my grandfather, 'come to see about the will of William Nantygors.'

'Come inside,' said the woman, and we went into the house where the upper half of a skeleton, with no ears and only a black hole for a nose, sat upright behind the yellow window.

The woman was William's daughter, Lwisa, who had come back from off to look after him, and because she had been pulling a fowl I could smell her long before I could see her in the dim passage. She and my grandfather stood whispering together a long time, they seemed to be plotting something, while I held tight to his tail with my heart thumping and the skin on my whole body gone too tight for me to breathe.

'Do you think he will last long now, Lwisa?' my grandfather asked her in a whisper. 'No, no,' she answered, 'that old owl was hooting outside again last night, and to-day two pictures fell off the wall.' – 'Fair play,' said my grandfather, 'and how will he take it, do you think, me coming over the doorstep of

Nantygors again after all these years?' – 'Don't you worry, Dafydd *bach*,' she answered, 'you and he were raised together and it's easy to light a fire on an old hearth when the grave is close by. We'll humour him and your six pounds will soon be safe in your pocket.'

My grandfather seemed to brighten up at that. 'Lwisa *fach*,' he said, dangling his bowler behind his back, 'there's see you changed I do. You are getting too fat to get in your coffin, girl,' and he butted her towards the door with his big belly. They both laughed and we all went together into the back-kitchen, a small room lit by a miserable half candle standing in its own grease on the Bible and the ready-reckoner by the window.

The air in the room was thick with the smell of soot and sickness, you could cut it and it would open by itself like liver. There was a wooden four-poster bed without any frill or curtains to it in one corner of the room and, as I went forward in the gloomy half-light, I fell over the branch of a tree lying right across the bare flag-stones, with one end of it smouldering in the bottom of the grate, where there were a few cinders glowing like a widow's fire. The whole place was thick with grey dust and full of heavy cobwebs, the room was everywhere festooned with them like a disused cowshed, they were like hangings of grey cheese-cloth draped from the ceiling and fastening all the furniture to the walls. The only clear place in the room was the track from the door to the fireplace and to the shiny armchair that old William had kept clear with his daily movements, when he still had his legs under him. Everywhere else, over the pictures, and the dresser, and the fox in the case on the mantelpiece, were spread the grimy muslins of the cobwebs, thick with dust. The only bit of light in the room, too, was from that stump of candle stuck in front of the paper blind, the part nearest the window and the head of the bed was light – that was all; the rest of the room was gloomy and the spanish-brown walls were deep in shadow. You could tell how mean old William was by that, and by his working boots under the bed, tied up with white binder-twine instead of leather laces.

At first I was too terrified to look into the bed; I glanced everywhere with my heart thumping, around at the dusty grandfather's clock with the stopped hands dividing the face at six, and up at the bunches of bogbean and the sides of fat bacon thick with dust hanging out of the cobwebs from the butcher's hooks in the ceiling. I was afraid if I looked I was going to see the bone ribs like ladder-rungs, and the chalky skull on top of them with the bare teeth chattering, the upper half of a skeleton sticking out of the bedclothes in the candle-light.

But soon I saw William wasn't a real skeleton after all, although he was very skinny. He didn't say anything when we went in, he just lay there very drowsy, wearing a nightgown made out of a dark brown flour-sack with a hole slit in the bottom for his head to come through, and the corners cut off for his arms, he was propped up stiff against the pillows of his four-poster with his eyes shut and his long arms, bare and bony, spread out over the dark bedclothes. His fierce face was thin and whitish in the candle-light, and hung with sagging festoons of loose skin, there was no meat on his bones, and the loose folds and wrinkles of skin draped under his eyes and over his cheek-bones were caught back, like window curtains, each side of his toothless mouth, and his long neck was thin and skinny like the neck of a turkey. He was quite bald and his head was shiny, and climbing up across his white temple was a prominent zigzag vein, a bluish twisting tube looking as though a buried blue-bodied worm had burrowed its way in under his glistening skin already. He had no hair and no moustache, but his eyebrows were stiff and heavy, and because he hadn't shaved there was a faint sparkle to his jaws and his chin. He had changed a lot since I saw him last and he was for the worms now I could see, but I couldn't take my eyes away after looking at him. I was fascinated by the hanging skin of his savage face and the thick blue blood-vein going zigzag up over his shiny temple.

William's short daughter brought the polished armchair to the bedside for my grandfather. Then she got another chair for herself, dusted it and sat down on it, lifting me on to her canvas apron. I didn't like her doing that, I wanted to be the other side of the bed by my grandfather. And besides, she had such a big swollen bust and such a shallow lap that I kept sliding off her knees all the time, and my trousers were soon cutting me hot between my legs like cheese-wire. She was a short stout woman, bosomy, with small feathers in her hair and on her black flannel blouse from plucking the chicken, and all the time her face was a dull glowing red as though she had just come upright from a bending position. But the funniest thing about her was her mouth, because her wide-spaced teeth were set at right angles to her gums, they splayed out between her rubbery lips like the stubs of a bunch of bananas.

For a long time we all sat there in dead silence, the skeleton in the bed, my grandfather with his belly in his lap and a holy expression on his face, and Lwisa on the border of her chair, nearly pushing me off her apron with her heavy breathing. She didn't so much sit as hook the spare fat of her rump on to the edge of the seat, and every now and then her rough hands would begin searching in my hair. Because the clock had stopped the room was as silent as the grave, except that somewhere a watch was beating like a small heart, and from time to time the grit in the candle wick would splutter like a pinch of toenails sprinkled on the fire.

Then at last old William began to chew the insides of his dry cheeks, altering the folds of skin upon his toothless face, like the wrinkles moving on a pig's bladder when you begin to blow it up with a straw. And slowly lifting his thin lids he turned his face on the pillows to Lwisa and spoke in his heavy bass voice. His eyes under their stiff straw-like eyebrows were black and fierce, but bright, they shone like a shop-lamp from his dead face, and I jumped to hear such a deep voice come out of the sitting bones.

'Lwisa,' he said, 'is there a drop of cold water in that cup by your elbow?'

'Yes, father,' she answered, very religious, 'will you have some now?'

She pushed me off her lap to help the old man to drink the water, as fussy as a hen with one chick, but closing his eyes again he said, 'No, *I* don't want it, but your tongue is sure to be dry with all the talking you've done to me this evening.'

Her hot face went red as a toasting fire and she smiled sheepishly, showing her teeth like a bit of machinery; she took the hint and began to explain she had brought her father's old friend and neighbour to help him make his will.

'Who is it?' he asked.

'Dafydd Penry the carpenter,' she answered, winking at my grandfather.

The old man opened his eyes and shot her an angry glance that missed her and went right through my shirt and into my heart. 'Dafydd Penry,' he growled. 'I'd see him coke first. A man who could jew a neighbour out of fifty yards of galvanized wire! If he is here, he had better put his foot to the earth fast, or I will get off my deathbed and turn him over the threshold of Nantygors myself.'

There was a lot of wrangling then between Lwisa and William, with my grandfather joining in now and then trying to keep the dish steady between them, with his little herbal head steaming. I couldn't understand all of it, but in the end they got the old man to agree to draw a line under their quarrel and to let my grandfather make his will. 'You must learn to forgive, my father,' Lwisa kept on saying, pulling me back on to her knees again, 'you must learn to forgive.'

'All right,' he answered, 'I'll forgive him because I'll soon have the big stone over me, but there's no need for you to forgive him, mind, Lwisa. If I thought you had forgiven him I wouldn't leave you a red penny, remember.'

'No, no, of course not,' she answered as she nodded and winked at my grandfather, who was sitting the opposite side of the bed again glazed after shaving and like a dark toby jug with the top off.

Then old William began saying what he wanted done.

'The elbow, Dafydd Penry,' he said, 'is nearer than the wrist, and although the children have quarrelled with me I don't want a lot of old strangers who speak English and wear rubber heels to handle my money. So put it down that the money is to be shared between the children.'

'Very good,' said my grandfather, bladdering the long pod of his nose into his handkerchief and then writing in the little book. 'Very good indeed. But, William, don't you think Lwisa ought to have a little bit more than the others? She is the one who has come back to you in the days of your tribulation.'

The old man looked steadily at him with his hooded eyes, and then began scratching at his knee-bones as though a worm was already eating its way in there. 'All right,' he said, in his gruff voice, 'she shall have the gold watch and guard off the dresser there, instead of Johnny Emlyn. He is not a quarter right, poor dab, and he doesn't know how to use one yet.'

'Not a quarter right!' said my grandfather with a crafty look, soaping the old man up as fast as he could. 'Not a quarter right! He's not a half right, and from the way he has treated you he doesn't deserve anything, the scamp. Why don't you leave his share to Lwisa altogether?'

The old man sat nibbling at this for a bit, casting suspicious glances at Lwisa and my grandfather all the time, and looking every now and then as though he was going to come to the boil again. But after a bit of arguing and coaxing they got him to agree to it, and then they went on in the same way for a long time, saying not to leave anything to Thomas Henry because he had a curl in his tail; and giving to William Francis would be like carrying water over the river, because he had any amount already; and since Marged Elin went in with the bread and came out with the buns it was best not to trust her with money now, poor thing; until the old man seemed to be leaving nearly everything he had to Lwisa.

But I was dead tired by this; every time I moved, my eyes bobbed to and fro in my head with wearinesss and bad air and at last, in spite of my cutting trousers, I began to doze. I didn't want any rocking that night and soon I was fast asleep on Lwisa's lap.

I don't know how long I slept there on those short thighs, but I woke abruptly when Lwisa threw me into the foot of the four-poster. There was a riot in the room and I saw her springing forward to hold old William down in bed. 'I've had a bellyful of this. No cup will hold more than a cupful,' he was shouting, trying to get at my grandfather with his claws and shaking the loose skin and pouches of his face. 'I'll do what I like with the money, Dafydd Penry,' he yelled. 'Leave you six pounds for the grandson, indeed! I'll settle who's to have the money. Who's dying, me or you, you scoundrel?'

He struggled so hard his eyes went into a bad squint and the blue blood-vein in his head swelled up to such a size I thought it was going to burst. He seemed to lose all his weakness, he was shouting and tossing his scarecrow arms about so that Lwisa and then my grandfather had to hold him down fast by the nightshirt and the ankle, while the bedclothes overflowed on to the flagstones. 'But fair play, father, fair play,' Lwisa pleaded. 'Dafydd Penry must have something for his trouble. He must live, like all of us.' – 'Live,' the old man howled back at her. 'Live, did you say? Dafydd Penry will live where the crows will die, so don't you worry about him living.'

'Leave upsetting him, Lwisa *fach*, leave upsetting him,' said my grandfather, pulling the bedclothes back over old William's feet. 'Always best to pat the head of a wicked dog. Die now, little William,' he went on soothingly, 'everything is settled, so die now tidy for me and Lwisa, there's a good boy.' Gradually the old man became exhausted again, and soon the uproar was over. While Lwisa dried the sweat off his head I fell fast asleep again, seeing first my grandfather winking and tucking his rubber front back into his waistcoat after the struggle.

When I awoke the second time everything seemed different. The fire had gone out and there wasn't a sound in the room. I looked up towards the top of the bed and there was Lwisa tying her father's jaw up with a piece of pudding-cloth, and in the corner shadows by the dresser was my grandfather in his shirtsleeves, trying on a new pair of trousers over his corduroys. I saw him take his eyes out of the corners. 'Do you think he's gone, Lwisa?' he whispered.

'He ought to be,' she answered, 'I've held his mouth closed long enough. But I can't get this cloth to stay round his head.' As she tried, her teeth-ends showed out through the mound of her lips.

My grandfather came prancing into the candle-light, wearing the brand-new pair of trousers, too long in the leg and too tight round the middle. He drank up the brandy and the jug of bogbean off the table and then, sidling up to Lwisa with his white fang grinning, and giving her a dig with his elbow, he said, 'What about the six pounds, Lwisa?'

'Very good, Dafydd,' she whispered, 'you tie him up and I'll feel under the mattress for the stocking.'

I knew old William was dead but I was too tired to care. I lay half dozing in the foot of the four-poster and saw my grandfather go to William's hard bald skull, that was shining in the candle-light smooth and hard as a bubble of glass, with the blue tube still to be seen in it. I saw him tying his jaw up with the grey rag, and bragging to Lwisa that he could always tell at once if a customer was dead or not by the feel of the gums, even Didi Gai, who was fat as a breeding-sow and still warm three days before the funeral when he went to deliver her coffin, because the hot weather and her feather bed had kept her heat in under her.

Then as he was finishing his job Lwisa groped out a long black woollen stocking with a white toe from under the mattress and held it up, while the two of them grinned at each other, one each side of the bed, showing their different teeth. The next moment they were in the shadows by the dresser with their backs to me, my grandfather's little head so queer it looked as though a heavy blow had hammered it flat. They were there a long time, whispering and laughing quietly, and at last I heard my grandfather dropping coins into his hand, counting out his sovereigns in a loud and cheerful voice: '. . . One,' he said proudly, 'two – three – four – five – six.'

But the moment he finished counting there was a tremendous crash of thunder that shook the house from its foundations to its eaves and gutters, the yellow spire of flame on the candle cowered with the shock, and the whole dusty room trembled violently on its foundations, as though it had been almost bumped over by the charge of a powerful row of bulls. Lwisa and my grandfather stood stock still waiting for silence again in the quaking house but, before they could move, the grand-father's clock in the corner began slowly striking as though it would never stop, it crashed out the strokes at the top of its hoarse voice, retching and making dry noises among the wheels and chainwork of its unoiled inside, and finishing the sixth stroke with a deafening crash that sounded as though it had smashed its inside to pieces, beginning with the broken bell. Strike – strike – strike – strike – strike – strike – and outside the pouring rain hissed down suddenly in tons around the hollow house.

Lwisa and my grandfather looked at each other and then turned together towards the head of the bed. The way they stared, as though they had seen a roaring ghost, Lwisa with the whites of her eyes showing and my grandfather with his fat black underlip hanging out of his face like a windowsill, made me look, too, in the same direction. For a cold second I saw William with the pudding-cloth hanging in a loop on his chest and his black eyes wide open, he was staring straight before him at Lwisa and my grandfather, who were holding on to each other by the dresser. His white face seemed all skin against the rough brown sacking of his nightgown, his eyelids and his cheekbones were hung with sagging skin, and his scraggy chicken's throat had enough loose flesh for two necks hanging around it. But he was breathing, and his two black eyes under their thick thatch of eyebrows were wide open, watching the fat little figures by the dresser.

Then his wattles began to move, but before he could say anything my grandfather, the sweat like glass beads buried in his face, jumped with a loud yell out of the shadows and, snatching me off the foot of the bed, dragged me towards the door of the kitchen. But in his hurry he forgot the tree-branch lying across the floor, and it tumbled him over with a heavy thud, so that he lay kicking like a black beetle on his back. And before we could scramble out of the room we saw Lwisa collapsed in the armchair with her eyes going round and round in her head; and old William sitting down on the kitchen flag-stones in his nightshirt, pulling his boots on with his claws.

When we flung open the back door we heard the loud roar of the rain like a thousand rooks rising and the night was pitch black before us, it was like looking into a dark cupboard, but we dashed without stopping out into the yard in the pouring weather. As we splashed our way forward through the deep mud, the thunder would pound the heavens above us, and big sheets of lightning would drop out of the sky in one piece, lighting up the pouring rain. But we didn't wait to shelter although we were soon soaking wet, all we wanted was to get away from Nantygors as fast as we could. We hurried forward, my grandfather in his bowler-hat and his shirt-sleeves, stopping his trot every few yards to hitch up William's trousers that were dragging in the mud. We splashed our way on, passing close to old Phylip Wernddu, who was singing a hymn of thankfulness under his umbrella on his way home from chapel. But the night was black as a bull's belly and he didn't see us, and soon we reached the stone stile.

There, just as we were crossing over, we saw William Nanty-gors by a flash of lightning, standing outside the house on the edge of the bog in his boots and the boiled bag of his nightshirt. He was tall and narrow, like a long-legged scarecrow in the pouring rain, with his thin head, and his skinny arms showing out of the corners of his black nightgown. In his hand was the long stocking, and by the next flash of lightning we saw it sailing out over the bog, the golden coins from it in a shower in the lightning as they scattered flashing over the muddy land.

I looked at my little grandfather and he was crying steadily in the darkness beside me, he was sitting on top of the stone stile in his shirt-sleeves and his bowler-hat, crying, with the rain pouring over him.

'What's the matter, Dadcu?' I asked him. 'What are you crying for?'

'It's my six sovereigns and my little book,' he sobbed aloud. 'I left them on the dresser and William has thrown them into the bog.'

'Never mind,' I said, trying to comfort him, 'we'll make another will somewhere else soon. Perhaps for Mari Cyn Adda – she isn't looking very healthy these days.'

'Never again,' he said, 'never again. I have finished, and my fiddle is in the thatch. I ought to have seen that I could never get the better twice of William Nantygors. Everybody knows that even if the devil was on the other side of the broth-bowl William would get the dough-boys. Joseph *bach*, I ought to have known better.'

He sat there crying in the thunder and lightning and I couldn't get him to budge, until at last the hailstones tapping at his bowler-hat, and a wind like the cold coming under the door, made him start trotting home again.

It rained hard all night, and the next morning we heard that with the flooding of the stream Nantygors, and everything in it, had gone under the mud.

PRICE-PARRY

Snow and darkness lay thick over Llanifor Fechan and all the boots in the village were under the beds. Suddenly night came off the sky like a shirt, and a vast red orb of sun rose up intolerant and masterful above the earth, watching the world from the back of the mountain. It glared down upon the sweep of snowy landscape, upon the ring of hills black with stiff trees like wooden hairs, and on the pan-shaped hollow in the middle of the white fields, where the village chimneys began to steam up into the morning. The earth turned colour under the ruddy gaze, and the houses caked in the bottom of the pan were transfigured. The panes of the hill-side vicarage blazed like slabs of pure copper; Glandwr's unsoiled roof was pink and on the sills of the little windows were wedges of pinkish snow; and the tumble-down cottage of Mati Tŷ-unnos blushed in the glare of the sunrise, its low and scabby walls bulging outwards like the wallow of a bitch in heavy whelp.

And when the whole land was lighted, another orb rose in counter arrogance to the west of the village, as majestic and domineering as the first, and almost as all-seeing, it too exalted itself and looked out in rival possessiveness and mastery over the snow-clad scene. It was the blue eye, cold and blue as ice-water, of the Reverend Roderick Pari Pryce Price-Parry, son of the sons of Rhodri Mawr, Vicar of Llanifor Fechan, surmounting at daybreak the shawl-fringe of his four-poster to find if this were burial weather. Seeing the snow still thick it stopped. The hill-side graveyard would be bitter cold. With grandeur in its sweep, the icy eye-ball and its blue fellow blazed at the silver watch hung on a horse-nail hammered into the wooden bedpost. It was time to rise. As the tall vicar put on his dark clothes he saw the village below him steam like a vomit, and the black reaping-hooks of his eyebrows contracted. He turned away, thinking of his tree and the paintings fastened upon his parlour wall.

On the boards of Geta Glandwr's bedroom hung a little mirror framed with plush and cockleshells, and as she woke with her mother's shout she saw the risen sun's reflection glowing in the glass like a ball of molten bronze. She sat up in her night-dress watching, and heard a gambo-wheel crack outside, a dog and a cock bark and crow together, and then the ring of the thick milk belling into the pail. She scrambled out of bed, said her prayers, and looked from the window down into the farm-yard below. There was interlacing snow on the orchard boughs like a white shawl of thick knitting laid over the trees in one piece. The cartshed, left open all night, had a strip of snow along the top of the door, and leaning against the white-thatched rick was a ladder with snow on every rung. It would be cold leading the vicar's horse to the graveyard. Geta shivered at the thought of it, as though a snowflake had fallen into her ear.

The hanging blood-ball showed itself hot too at the one-pane window of old Mati Tŷ-unnos. But she did not look at it, or rise, or care a scratch how chill the day was going to be. She was lying cold and still. She was lying dead.

The vicar stood with his back to the empty fire-place, staring about at his bare kitchen, small, cold and comfortless in the gloom. It was half underground, built like a kind of stone cellar into the hill at the back of the vicarage, and the small window was up near the ceiling. Moisture ran down the unwiped walls as though they were the sides of a vault. Large thick slabs of blue slate with black warts growing out of them paved the floor. There was a shelf for boots over the back door where a pair of waders hung from a cup-hook, and a thick wooden peg was driven into the chimney wall to hold the pony's harness. On the bare plank table beneath the dim light of the window lay a broad-brimmed clerical hat, and a large black cloak was piled on the seat of the armchair alongside it. The hat had a round disc of grease on the top, as though all the fat of the vicar's body was slowly oozing out through the top of his head.

Large and ominous in the gloom, Price-Parry shivered on the hearthstone in his ancient clothes. Even the back of his tongue felt cold, and he was rubbing his hands together to try to warm them. His fingers were large and knuckly, the big nails flat and yellow like sheets of thin horn. He was a very tall bony man, bow-backed and eagle-beaked, his out-thrust face ecclesiastical brass and his white hair, parted in the middle, drooping in a curve on each side of his head like the pages of a Bible open at the 97th Psalm. His yellow features were covered with smooth book-skin, and bending from his jawbone down into his clerical collar were two or three ribs of loose flesh like the curved vaulting of a church roof. As he waited for Geta he saw the mocking face of Mati Tŷ-unnos before him, refusing to call him 'sir', and his fierce blue eyes blazed round in indignation at the boot-rack, and the wood of the armchair like streaky bacon, and the rusty duck-gun leaning against the streaming wall.

Soon there came a knock at the kitchen door, and when Price-Parry had shouted, 'Come in', he heard a kicking noise outside as Geta knocked the snow off her clogs before entering the house. When she came in, the waders swung to and fro in the dimness behind the door, and at once she remembered how the first time she entered the gloomy kitchen she ran out again screaming, because the sight of those feet not reaching the slate slabs made her think the vicar had hanged himself from the bacon hooks.

As she stood demurely before the towering vicar she was small and dainty, she seemed light and birdlike, as though she might at any moment begin hopping or pecking under her armpits. She had a small white face as compact as the face of a watch and two curved hair-slabs of gold met along the middle of her head. She wore a thick grey overcoat made prettily out of a blanket with a belt and bright stripes on it as blue as grass. She had her thick black working stockings on and her canvas apron showed below the hem of her overcoat.

Geta was a kind-hearted girl, and for months she had gone daily into Mati's cottage to look after her in her last illness. As she stood before the black and yellow vicar, looking so handsome to her now because he was cold, she said, 'Good-day, if you please, sir,' and dropped him a curtsey. He swung his fierce bird-head from side to side before replying, and then pulled the skin back off his yellow teeth. They were large and three-cornered, the points fastened up in the gums. 'Good-day, good-day,' he said, staring down hard at her in his overbearing fashion. When the vicar stared, Geta noticed, he did not so much slide back his lids as push his eye-balls farther out of the bones of his face. But he hardly saw her, thinking how Mati Tŷ-unnos, who had thwarted and provoked him so long, was now lying dead, and within an hour or two would be buried for ever.

The thought pleased him. He smiled again. He would show this child his tree. 'Margaretta,' he shouted down at her, 'have you heard about my tree?' – 'Yes, if you please, sir,' she answered curtseying once more. 'Everybody has heard about your tree, sir.' Price-Parry dropped his lip back over his teeth. 'Would you like to see it?' he threatened. 'Yes, if you please, sir,' said Geta.

Leaving the dim cellar he led the way through the passage to the front of the house and Geta slipped off her clogs to follow him. In the darkened parlour his boots creaked about as though they had been by the fire, but at last he divided the curtains a bit and let a thin sheet of icy white sunlight into the room. Geta stood like spoon-food outside the busy mouth, waiting patiently to be invited into the shadowy room, making out the desk in the darkness, and the books with shields on them lining the walls, and the big picture covered with sacking that reached almost from the floor to the ceiling.

'Come in and stand here,' he commanded, pointing with the stiff twigs of big fingers to a bald spot in the carpet in front of the picture. Geta crept in on feet soft as rabbit-pads and stood on it. Price-Parry had a bright seat to his serge as he bent down in the sunshine and rolled the long piece of canvas up off the picture.

Near the bottom, by the thick frame, Geta saw a stiff man very much like the vicar lying on the ground wearing an overcoat but no trousers. There was a hole in the breast of his coat and into this disappeared the bark-covered roots of a tree. The rest of the picture was packed with leafy branches on which hung names and little paintings like square fruit. The vicar told Geta the man lying down on the ground was Rhodri Mawr, King of the Kymry, and the little pictures showed the gold-gowned fathers of Price-Parry marrying, ruling and killing one another. He smiled and rubbed his hands together, a little warmer now even in a house where the crack of a fire was never heard, as the slice of sunlight made the little paintings glisten.

Geta stood, not looking at the tree, watching the vicar, with her coat open and her hands under her canvas apron. 'Do you like it?' he said, creaking like upholstery as he moved about in his stiffness. 'Look, this is Griffith Frith, lord of the top half of our parish. And here on the lowest branches, where the tree divides, are the six sons of Rhodri Mawr. Can you see them from there?'

'Not very well, if you please, sir,' she said.

He came back and stood close to her, his peering face out-thrust and the skin of it yellow over the bird-bones.

'Twti down a bit,' he said doubtfully.

She twtied.

Then with loud cracks he bent low himself until his head was nearly resting on the floor. She could see his flannel shirt inside his gaping collar, and the crop of warts on the front of his neck, each with a little bow of cotton tied round it.

'This one here,' he went on, getting up again and going back to the picture, 'is Griffith Benfras. This one is Ifor ap Cynan ap Maredudd ap Rhisiart. And here at the very top of the tree,' he cried, getting on to a chair and pointing triumphantly to a name near the ceiling, 'is Meurig ap Rhys Goch, my great-great-great-great-grandfather.' He sneezed like glass smashing and then turned round. 'What are you twti-ing down for?' he asked. 'If you please, sir, you told me to, sir,' she replied, looking up at him. He scowled, coughed and took out his silver watch. 'Harness the pony,' he commanded. 'I shall be with you in two minutes.' He got down off the chair frowning. Geta straightened herself and crept silently out of the room to harness the pony.

The vicar sat upright in his high-wheeled cart, wearing his waders, his black hat and his big cloak, gazing out over the snow-clad country with the glance of a bird of prey. His breath floated about, blown over his face like fine powder as his stare dominated the white fields, and the weak sun that was now dissolving above them like a lump of pale butter. Before him marched the stiff-limbed ginger-bread pony, his thick unclipped hair standing out at right-angles to his skin and his frozen legs unbending at the knee-joints. Geta trudged through the snow holding his bridle. 'A little child shall lead them,' murmured Price-Parry, as he spread out his cloaked arms like a king on the seat each side of him.

Geta too looked about her as she went along at the pony's head, seeing the starlings hopping like flocks of rabbits on the white slopes, and a bramble-bush rising low off the field as though it were the bones of a snow-buried skeleton. She thought of old Mati Tŷ-unnos, soon to be buried, and cried a little to herself with cold and grief. She pondered on the walk she had done every morning to Mati's tiny cottage, which had a curved red horn of a chimney, and scabby white-washed walls like flesh with a poultice just taken off, and an overgrown thatched roof gay as a garden in summer with foxglove, and willow herb and dandelion. Morning after morning old Mati had lain in bed until Geta got there, her foot cold as though it had stood in the river, watching the black stump of her bandages take shape against the glow or primrose of her one-pane window. Under the thick blankets she was a swollen load, heavy, a bedful, a big spreading old woman with a long egg-like face showing over the quilt-edge, her skin covered with a tangle of little lines and cracks like the cheek of an old broth basin. She wore a couple of firm grey plaits, wool-wound at the ends, over the bedclothes, and on the top of her head was a greasy black felt hat with crimson pork-scorings down the crown, and a glass-headed hatpin stuck through it, glistening white as a glassy eyeball fixed unblinking on the morning. She had learnt to keep dead still at night because every time she shifted the brass balls fell off the bed-posts into the bed.

As Geta cleaned and fed her they talked of her repentance, and of the time before that when Mati had a little grey donkey, and a flat two-wheeled cart, and earned her living by carrying the farmers' eggs and rabbits up to market. Shâms Bach was so small his four little shoes wouldn't cover your hand and the people used to say that when he fell down ill in the field, poor dab, Mati carried him into the kitchen in her apron to give him a cup of small beer. And they used to say, too, that once, when Mati had had a skinful, she rolled to the back of the cart and her weight hoisted the little animal right up off the road. But she was loath to tell Geta that, or that a few times she had stood before her betters in the court, or that once or twice a low-flying baby had happened to fall into her lap. She was only a repentant and balloon-legged old woman now, whose toes every morning were cold as icicles until the passing sun shone into her cottage and warmed her bandaged foot, so that it began to smoke like a steam pudding before the window.

'Geta,' she said, when she knew she could not last much longer, 'I am not afraid to cross the Jordan now, after what you have told me and read to me. On the other side there are not only black marks against us in the big book, there is a big ginger-rubber there too to rub them out, isn't there?'

'That's right, Mati,' said Geta. 'If we repent we will be forgiven everything.'

Mati considered a bit, wearing on the long egg of her face her little glasses with brass frames.

'It won't matter if I can't speak much of that old English there, will it, Geta? Indeed now.'

'No, no, not at all,' Geta told her. 'But go to sleep, there's a good girl, or you won't feel worth a roast potato.'

'I will do whatever you tell me, and I thank providence fifty times a day for you, my sweetheart,' she answered.

In the mind of the vicar too ran the thoughts of old Mati. He sat brooding in his cart, his head outstretched on the long bony neck that looked as though it had lost its feathers, and the wind splitting against the edginess of his beaked nose as the river divides at the sharp pillars of the village bridge. He recalled how she had always jeered at him and made sport of him, and the thought of it knitted the black sickles of his meeting brows. One blazing hot day, he remembered, he had caught her up driving Shâms Bach to market wearing a grey shawl and a hat with a new red ribbon. On the cart was a butter tub with the unprotected butter running like water in the heat and leaking out all over the cart. As he passed her she called after him. 'Vicar,' she shouted, sounding as though she had stopped very often after leaving Llanifor Fechan. 'Vicar, there's proud you are. Where are you going to?'

'I'm walking to market,' he said shortly. 'The pony has cast a shoe.'

'For the sake of everything, jump up here,' she shouted, patting the box she was sitting on.

He looked down from his great height at Shâms Bach but he did not reply. Every night as he put his head to the pillow of his four-poster he heard the blue blood of Rhodri Mawr march past his ears. Soon his long legs had carried him ahead. 'Are you ashamed of the little donkey?' she shouted after him. 'There's no need for you to be. Your Master rode on the back of one of these.'

The vicar took off his hat and shook his lion-locks at the remembrance of it. Mati Tŷ-unnos, the by-blow, the bush-begotten, the chance-child, and the mother of chance-children. Even now on his way to bury her the thought of her transgressions against his pride tasted bitter in his belly. When her second child came he went to the little cottage to speak to her about the baptism. There was the thatched roof in full bloom, and the little shaggy rick in the yard looking as though it wanted to scratch itself against the wall, and Shâms Bach to be seen through the window in the field outside, with a tremendous crow standing outspread on his little back. Mati was sitting by the fire giving suck to the child because Wil Saer was there putting a new leg in the stool.

'William,' bawled Price-Parry coming down the path. 'Leave off your hammering. I want to talk to Mati Rees.'

'Yes, sir; at once, sir,' said Wil. He touched his cap and went out the back way. He was a heavy man, with thick fluffy moustaches that covered his mouth and had taken root in his cheeks.

'So you've got a new baby again,' said Price-Parry standing in the low doorway, the fierce bird-bones of his head hung forward into the kitchen. Mati smiled up at him. 'That's how it is,' she said. But although the kite-eyes were masterful upon her she was cool, she didn't alter a feather.

'Is it a boy or a girl?' he thundered.

'Give a guess,' she answered at once. He was taken aback. He frowned. He saw Wil Saer safe outside grinning in through the back window.

'A boy, a boy,' he guessed impatiently.

'No!' she replied. 'Give another guess.'

'Well, a girl,' he shouted back at her.

'Ay, how did you know then? You must be a wise-man, or somebody told you.' She smiled up at him again with her long-fleshed face.

He warned and denounced her with all the power of his mouth, crying woe from the doorway upon her fornications and debaucheries until the baby began to howl. 'Put that child back on the breast,' he shouted, coming at last to Rhodri Mawr, his little pictures and his tree. But at that she lost her temper. 'It's a pity you haven't got a photo of your Uncle Roderick on your

old tree,' she shouted back at him, 'getting out of his carriage
to throw my grandfather and all us children out of Parcau Bach
on to the road, the endless tyrant. Get out of here, get out, get
out, Price-Parry,' she screamed, 'or I'll break your back with a
pole.'

But to-day Mati Tŷ-unnos lay quiet in her coffin, the body
that had known the sweat of lechery was at last at rest, having
reaped in reward for its sinfulness, corruption, and a leaking foot,
and death. In half an hour it would be all over. He saw the
church spire over the snowy hedges close ahead with the green
cock still crowing into the east.

Snow lay all over the grass and the tombstones, and the
daylight was beginning to fail on the countryside. In the middle
of the graveyard rose the little church with a light burning in
the vestry window, and around it stood a grove of bare trees
like the picked black bones of a monster.

Geta crouched holding the pony's head, and watching the
burial over the low cemetery wall. She saw the vicar reading the
service at the graveside, while a small group of people in gloves
and overcoats stood beside him listening. She was too far off to
hear what he was saying, but as he spoke he huddled down low
on the earth, pointing into the hole, and then rose like a great
white bird to his full height. Would he take off Geta wondered,
would wings leap from his shoulders and bear him out of sight
over the church and the trees? He fluttered down to his normal
size again. Soon he turned away and strode back to the little
church to change, while the handful of mourners, touching their
hats, moved off towards the graveyard gate. Mati Tŷ-unnos
was buried.

Geta crouched from the cold against the stonework, hoping
the vicar would not be long. The daylight was becoming dim,
and when she peeped over the wall to see if he was coming the
vestry light seemed brighter, more intense. The red pony began

plucking grass out of the mortar, and while she waited she
played idly with some pale snail-shells striped like peppermint
humbugs that she found in a hole in the wall. Suddenly she
awoke with a start. The vicar in his black clothes, wearing
around his neck a wide collar of his own breath, was bending
down and shaking her by the shoulder. 'Margaretta, Margaretta,' he was shouting. 'Get up into that cart at once. God
forgive me, I mean will you please get up into the cart, my
child?' He pushed her up the iron step and guided her gently
into her place, and then flicking the reins sat down on the seat
beside her. The pony moved off willingly down the lane. The
vicar's blue eyes glittered, his bare skin gleamed like backing-
silk. He looked very queer to Geta, warmer than he had ever
looked before. Had he been drinking in the vestry she wondered,
or was he saved? He drove the red horse along the snowy lane
laughing and murmuring to himself.

'"Repeat or repent," she said to me, Geta,' he muttered,
spreading his great baggy cloak out over her shoulders. ' "Repeat or repent, Roderick," she said to me. "You are an old
man, your time is short now. Do not drown three inches from
the shore. Show you have gathered wisdom and not only warts
on your skin." ' He laughed like a narrow bottle filling up with
water.

Geta was afraid to ask him whom he was speaking about.
Why was he laughing and sitting up here beside her with his
arm around her when, like a mangy king as Mati called him,
he always wanted to be led about the roads to every marriage
and burial in the parish? From the narrow of her eye he looked
thin, flushed and handsome to Geta. Perhaps he was ill or
beginning to be queer. At last she said to him – 'Please tell me
who you are talking about, sir.'

He turned his narrow face towards her. His nose under the
broad-brimmed hat was a blade, a curved out-bending blade
with a sharp edge to it. 'As I was taking off my surplice by the
candle,' he said, 'she oozed steadily through the vestry door like
the fog through a bare bush, she stood before me in the guise of

a great queen. "Mati," I said to her in my overbearing way, for which heaven forgive me, "Mati," I said, "beware, beware. I have just buried you legally, with reverence and holy writ. What do you want with me? Get back into your coffin at once, my girl." But I could see, Geta *fach*, she was not the same Mati as I had put safely under the ground. When I look out among the countenances of our short-legged peasantry, no, I mean among the faces of my countrymen, seldom do I encounter eyes on a level with my own. But this new Mati was a head taller than I am, she gleamed, she was pearlish with grandeur, and her form was phosphorescent in the yellow candle-light. She, with her dripping foot, and teeth in only the left-hand half of her mouth, and the big eyebrows of her long face up near her hair, you remember her Geta as she was, that body had shed its corruption and shone with glory, like the radiant cloths of the fuller.'

The repentance of Mati Tŷ-unnos was real then, and she after all had reached paradise. Had she a golden plate behind her head, Geta wondered. And had the vicar really spoken to her and she uprisen from her grave?

'Please, sir,' she said with great happiness, 'did you see Mati Tŷ-unnos in the vestry, and did she really speak to you?' The vicar nodded, showing his three-cornered teeth and squeezing her with his arm. 'Don't you believe me, Geta *fach*?' he asked.

'Oh yes, sir,' said Geta. 'She said that if ever by great grace and repentance she once managed to get her fingers up through the floorboards of heaven she would let me know somehow about it. And praise be she has.'

'She repented then, did she, Geta? That's why she said to me, "Vicar, repeat or repent." – "Your time is drawing near," she said. "Perhaps in a dozen spins of this old world from now the earth will be trickling on to your face through a crack in your coffin lid. So repent while there is yet time." But kicking against the pricks my stony heart spoke and may heaven forgive me for it. "What do you know of repentance, Mati Rees?" I asked her. "I don't suppose you could even spell the word."

She only smiled at me, Geta, she didn't shout "I wouldn't give
a hair from my nose to spell it," or some other rudeness as she
would have done but for grace. "Vicar *bach*," she said to me
patiently, "you don't understand not even rule one. Believe
what I tell you. I am not just breaking words but trying to save
you from your pride. When Geta read to me, struggling with
me day after day, as you should have done, at last I felt I was
forgiven; once it was as though a wing touched me and I
soared. And now by this victory I, Mati Tŷ-unnos, know all
secrets and mysteries, I have seen the nest of the stirring thunder,
the eyes that watch the nether sinks of hell, the knuckles that
wring out the showers and the storm of falling stars." Those
were her very words, Geta, she spoke them in a deep voice like
an organ-chord, towering above me in her shawl and poppy hat,
filling the vestry with her beanfield fragrance and her glow.'

By now the cart was out of the cemetery lane and on the road
back to the village. The frozen pony went easier, bending his
knees a bit because he knew he was heading for his oats. Geta
felt happy, in her heart the sun was on the hill. 'Let me get out
now and lead the pony, sir,' she said, 'and if you please, sir, tell
me what else she said.'

'You lead the pony? No, indeed,' said the vicar. 'I will lead
the pony.' He slipped off his cloak and wrapped it warmly round
her. Then with loud cracks he got out of the cart and took the
bridle, turning round and talking to Geta as he walked the road
towards the village.

'Her eyes, Geta,' he said, 'that were small and cunning, like
the black beady eyes of the bat you remember, were open wide
and shining brightly in her face. "I will tell you a secret I have
heard," she said to me. "I, whom you despised so much, I,
Mati Tŷ-unnos, was also a daughter of Rhodri Mawr, his blood
flowed in my veins too, I had as much right to be on your tree
as Griffith Benfras or Ifor ap Cynan. And what is more, Geta
fach Glandwr, she too is a child of the Great King; we are all
related, Vicar, and not in the ninth degree, neither." ' The
vicar stopped the cart. 'When I heard that, Geta, that she

whom I had hated so much was related to me, at first I couldn't breathe, my bones felt heavy as though they were going to fall out of my skin. But she was slowly melting out my frozen heart, may heaven be praised.' He lifted his hat off his white locks and started the pony again. ' "Beware of pride, Roderick Price-Parry," she said. "Beware of the vanity of that tree of yours. It is nothing, Vicar *bach*, only a bit of a show-on-a-shelf remember. Pluck out those roots that are eating into your heart." I knew what she said was true, Geta; I knew it was the truth, but I had to deny it. "Pride!" I said to her. "Pride! I have no pride. When I heard of the heathen knocking his forehead on the ground before his god, I, Roderick Pari Pryce Price-Parry, of the line of Rhodri Mawr, the very next Sunday got down full length before *my* God in this very church." You remember me doing that, Geta?' he asked turning round.

'Yes, sir,' said Geta, her hair protruding around her face like a curved golden shell, 'I remember you lying down flat in front of the altar to pray. Please won't you have your cloak on, sir?'

'No, indeed, Geta,' he said. 'I feel warmer leading this pony than I have been for years. Wrap it round you well, my child, to keep out the cold. Mati only smiled at my excuse. "Speak the truth, Vicar," she said, "and shame the devil; send a blush all over him right down to the spike of his tail. You know that as you lay there your heart was as cold as the stone of the steps beneath you." And what she said again was true, Geta.'

They reached the cottage of Wil Saer by the roadside. Wil was coming out of the gate of his little garden with a newly made cart-shaft over his shoulder. Seeing the vicar in his waders leading the pony down the road, and Geta sitting up there in the cart wrapped up in the black cloak, he dropped the shaft in the snow and clapped his hands to his furry face. He was just going to dodge back into the house when the vicar left the pony's head and ran down upon him, shouting at the top of his voice, so that the rooks smoked out of their trees, crying and floating about like bits of burnt paper from a chimney on fire. 'William, William,' he cried, holding him fast in his powerful eagle's claws, 'forgive me, forgive me. Will you forgive me, William? In my heart of hearts I despised you for years for being a carpenter and the son of a carpenter. If you can forgive me I shall be forgiven in heaven for forgetting my Master was the same. Can you forgive me, William?' the vicar shouted, gripping Wil's overcoat by the collar, and shaking him with his crooked yellow talons until Wil's red tongue shot out the length of a hand from among his plentiful moustaches. 'Yes, sir; yes, sir,' he gasped, frightened out of his life, crouching down with his elbows over his ears as though he was going to have a beating. 'Yes, sir, I'll forgive you anything, sir.' He fought himself loose and ran terrified through the tiny garden back to the house. 'Don't call me sir,' the vicar roared after him. But Wil was safe inside the house, and when he slammed the door all the snow fell off the roof on to the vicar. Price-Parry was too happy to notice. As he came back to the trap, tears gushed from his eyes. 'Geta,' he said, standing again at the gingerbread's bridle, 'Mati once said I never had any fires in my house because I was too high-nosed and proud to burn anything less grand than stars in my grate. Look out of your window to-night my girl and you will see smoke from every hearth in the vicarage. My uprooted tree and its pictures and its frame and every book about my tree and its pictures shall go up this night in smoke. Look out of your window, Geta *fach*, and see the flames.'

'Yes, sir,' said Geta, who sat watching wide-eyed from the cart with her mouth like a ball-hole. 'Thank you, sir. And please, sir, what became of Mati in the end?'

'I cannot tell you all she told me, Geta, you would not understand it. But I heard a line of music,' he said, 'something whistled as it whizzed past me, the vestry candle went out and she was gone.'

Through the darkness, the deserted cottage of Mati Tŷ-unnos semed more dilapidated than ever, its bulging walls crouching low in the snow. In the farmhouse of Glandwr Geta had climbed out of bed to stand at the landing window, staring in the direction of the vicarage. Presently, in the pitch night, she saw volumes of thick smoke pouring out of the chimney-stacks with a fiery glow glaring on it, as though all the chimneys of the house were on fire. Once or twice as she watched glove-fingers of flame showed themselves for a moment from the chimney-pots. Geta turned away smiling and crept back to her bedroom. Snow and darkness lay thick over Llanifor Fechan, and soon all the boots in the village were under the beds.

BOWEN, MORGAN AND WILLIAMS

After what I had done the night before I couldn't very well
refuse. Benja Bowen and I had come home from Imperato's
about nine o'clock, and I had gone straight into the front room
to slip my canvas boots into the window flower-pot with my
school cap on top of them, because my father didn't like me
going boxing. (I used to keep Benja's boots there too, because
his people were very strict and religious, much narrower than
mine – his father tried to start a sect that believed there were
thirteen Persons in the Trinity, and he made Benja go to chapel
on Saturdays.) There in the parlour my mother was sitting with
our new electric light on full-float, talking to two visitors from
our chapel – Miss Phillips (M'Liza, William the Rates's sister),
and Mrs. Rees the Come-inside, who had heard about her tumble. My mother was in her oil talking to them, she looked
beautiful with her crinkly auburny hair and the summerspots
on her eyelids, but she made me blush because she had her dress
on backwards. Mrs. Rees was a sour, knowing-looking woman,
red and stoutish, with a sultry expression on her face as though
she was having bad heart-burn. She had untidy grey hair like
the stuff that comes out of a rip in the sofa, and clothes that
seemed, if it wasn't for the heavy brooches she bolted them on
with, as though they were going to slide off her body. She had
on now her husband's panama hat with a barricade of hen's
feathers stuck upright into the ribbon, and a gnawed fur coat
hanging half-way down her back, the way our masters wore
their gowns. She kept an ironmongery shop, and everybody
called her the Come-inside because, if you stood looking in at
her window for a few seconds, she would waddle out on to the
pavement in her mangy coat and whisper, 'Come inside, come
inside.' She had a long stocking but she was stingey with her
money, and she and her husband lived in a little shed at the top
of the garden behind their mansion.

Miss Phillips, William's sister, was very genteel and polite, but poor-looking as well and very old-fashioned and dowdy. Summer and winter she wore a long voluminous greenish-black skirt, a riding coat of the same colour trimmed with wide braid like flat spanish, and a squashed velvet hat that looked as though she had found it under the cushion. I used to make fun of her with her elastic-sided boots and tall umbrella, and then be ashamed because really she was fine and I liked her very much. Her thin face was refined and white as ivory, very genteel, with a prim expression on it, because before William's leg got bad she used to be a governess.

I wanted to back out directly I had got inside the room, both because I had the boxing boots under my arm, and because I remembered in a flash that the mouthy Come-inside had seen Benja and me from her shed smoking up the mountain, where we used to go to shave each other, but it was too late.

'How do you do, Mr. Williams?' said Miss Phillips, holding out her thin white hand to me. (She was so polite she used to say 'Yes'm' and 'No'm' to my mother, and she started to call me mister as soon as I got into the county school.) I told her I was all right and I asked her how she was of course.

'Thank you for your kind enquiry,' she answered. 'If you mean my physical health, I am very well indeed. And now will you allow me to take this opportunity of congratulating you upon your recent success?'

I was taken aback for the moment, this speech seemed so elegant after Imperato's, but I realized she meant my passing senior at last. I blushed again and thanked her, but I was relieved to see the Come-inside looking as though her water-brash was a bit easier on her as she too wished me well. After a bit more handshaking amongst us, and dropping the boxing boots all over the floor, I got out into the cool passage.

I went into the kitchen, avoiding the puddles, and there Mam Evans, my mother's washer-woman, was crouching, eating toasted cheese out of a tin plate by the glow of the fire, because she was afraid to turn our electric light on. I did it for her, and then I sat down on the couch and began pumping her about the time she went on a trip to the seaside, and about her mother when she was a shindry girl. Mam Evans was a big fleshy old woman now, with a bun at the back of her head and a hot smell to her blouse. She had a soft shapeless face looking as though there were no bones in it, the flabby flesh beginning to hang into her goitrous neck, which was really a good bit wider than her head. There were no teeth or lips to her mouth, it was only a pleat in her skin right up under her nose. She couldn't see much with her pale watery eyes, so that my mother often had to wash the clothes over after her, and when she had scrubbed our kitchen floor she used to leave it swimming with puddles, with small heaps of brown snuff, like little molehills, scattered all over it.

When she had finished her cheese she took off her sack apron with the holes in the knees, and wrapped it in newspaper, asking me what time it was. I told her it was nine o'clock, and she swore in her faulty old-fashioned way because she would be too late to buy twist for her poor mother, alone in the dark house with an empty clay-pipe in her head. She hurried out the back way in her cap and shawl, and then I began to tease the canary a bit, hoping M'Liza and the Come-inside would go so that I could have my supper, but he was too sleepy to respond.

Then alongside my father's trombone in the corner I saw my mother's new vacuum cleaner, and I began examining that. I fixed a sort of plug with a wire on it into the wall, and then I turned on the current by means of a button I found under the handle. The engine started to hum, but almost at once there was a loud snap and a blue flash, and the electric light went out in the kitchen. I dropped the handle in my fright and then, when I had recovered a bit, I tried to put the light on at the switch, but nothing happened. I crept out of the kitchen in the darkness and tried the light in the middle room, but nothing happened there either. Just then my mother opened the door of the parlour, which I could see was also in complete darkness, and shouted out, 'Evan, Evan, now stop that nonsense. Put the lights on at once, will you!'

.   .   .   .   .

The next morning my mother's foot was a lot better and she said, 'Ev, take these roses up to your Uncle Sam's and ask how his asthma is, will you?' (She was holding the canary under the tap to revive him as she said this, because she had turned on the gas-ring and forgotten to light it, and the poor little dab had fallen off his perch in a faint.) The roses were all right, some of my father's best, each bloom bursting out like a coloured cabbage, and bound together into a huge bouquet nearly three feet in girth. But remembering the night before, and not being able to think of an excuse, I said I would go. So I heaved up the flowers off the table and started out the lane way to see my Uncle Sam, who lived the other end of the town.

Before I got to the main street I passed the Come-inside's husband on the prowl for back-rents, and the half-grin I fancied I saw on his face because of my flowers made me blush a bit. But I soon remembered seeing him looking silly in the big seat in chapel, with a white price-ticket, four inches by five, still sewn on the tail of his new frock coat, and that cheered me up again.

Before crossing over High Street I hung the flowers negligently half-way behind my legs to conceal them a bit and hurried over towards the tramroad, not looking to right or left. This tram-road ran parallel with the main street almost all the way to my uncle's house, and it wasn't bad walking there with no one about, and the sun yellow as electric light on the walls, although the place itself was shabby and dusty. The only thing that made me really uncomfortable was that my mother had been darning my socks again, and my right foot felt as though I had a poultice on it. My mother was lovely, with freckles and auburn hair, but it was wonderful my brother and I were still alive with all the things she had done to us. When our Rhysie was a baby, so she said, and she was tidying the dresser, she slipped him in the knife-drawer to answer Watcyn's the milk, and when she came back into the kitchen she began to search all over the place, behind the blower and in the boot cupboard, because she couldn't remember where she had put him.

At the back of the Temperance Hall I met Madame Jones-Edwards (Llinos Cwm Du, the majestic ex-singer) who had married three husbands, all of them little men about half her weight, each one before the last was cold. She was a tall stately woman leaning on an ebony walking-stick, wearing a white starched collar and a tie like a man, a costume of crimson plush, and a cartwheel hat with red seagulls skewered on to it. She rolled over slowly from side to side as she walked like a boy riding a bike too big for him. She was so sparkling and highly coloured, she looked a bit out of place on the grimy tramroad, which was only a narrow lane for the colliers' train, with the backs of shops and houses on each side of it. Her hands were covered with rings, there was a gold chain looped many times over her chest, and a long pair of droppers shaped like golden indian clubs swung on chains from the lobes of her ears. When she saw the roses she came slowly to rest upright, and asked me with an elegant sort of bow if she might smell them. She had a soft-skinned creamy face covered with fine lines as thin as hairs, and black bossy eyes, very glittering and watchful. The smell of the roses seemed to give her great raptures, she kept her face buried a long time in the massive bunch, closing her eyelids and letting her head loll on one side. She asked me where I had got them from and I thought she wanted to find out who I was too, but I didn't tell her much because she was so gushing, and I didn't know what she would do if she discovered my father played the trombone.

At last I got away, leaving even her scent behind, but I felt better after meeting her because these roses were silver bowl-winners after all, something to be proud of. My father grew about the best blooms in town, in the whole valley perhaps, and Llinos Cwm Du had liked them, and she had been all over the world singing in her young days, and had received bouquets too no doubt like the actresses Arthur and I saw in the Theatre Royal. She wasn't bad at all, except that she was too dramatic in everything she did, but you could see she was a good judge of roses, so that was nothing.

But when I came round the next bend I saw Arthur Vaughan Morgan crossing the tramroad on the way up from High Street, with his bull-terrier on the lead beside him. I dodged and marked time but it was no good, Arthur had seen me, and he was waiting with a faint smile on his face, looking at me as though I was something that had crawled out of the long grass. It was the same sort of look as he had for the kid who tagged on to us when we were small, the first day we were in the county school. 'Which way are you going?' Arthur said to him; 'we're going the other way.' He greeted me now with his lids half down over his deep blue eyes. 'Hullo, Williams,' he said, 'going to a wedding?'

When I told him I was on my way up to my Uncle Sam's, he said he would come with me after he had slipped home to give a message to his father. So for a start I had to carry my roses up to Arthur's house.

The first time I ever saw Arthur was when we were little boys and there was a coronation fête and gala on in town. I was with my father going among the crowds after the procession, and we met Arthur doing the same with *his* father, a well-known character the people called Tommy White-hat. The first thing I noticed about Arthur was that he had a much better Union Jack than I did, with a real gilded wooden point on the end of his flag-stick, and not a bit of pointed cardboard like mine. He was dressed in a sailor suit with long trousers and a thick white whistle-cord hanging out of his pocket.

His father was a tall big man wearing pale spats, a white fetl hat pushed on the side of his head, and a thin grey suit with lapels to the waistcoat and a scarlet carnation in the buttonhole. He was smoking a thin cigar like a pencil which he was using to point with, and which he kept passing from hand to hand as he made jokes and explained things to Arthur and me, bending down with his bright eyes close to mine and his breath smelling of scented cachous. He had a gold band on one of his fingers with a little hailstone in it, and he laughed and talked all the time in a rich-sounding way, showing a lot of gold in his big teeth. I thought him lovely then, with his mannish smell, and his handsome pink cheeks, and his thick curly hair like grey tobacco.

When Arthur and I got to the county school Mr. Vaughan Morgan always talked to me in a grown-up way, and asked about my mother and father in his rich throaty voice, very cheerful and friendly. I always thought then he came right off the top shelf, but whenever I mentioned him at home my mother would turn on me and say, 'Hark at him, he likes Tommy Vaughan Morgan who feeds the children on bread and spit, and works his poor Annie's hands into holes so that he can live among the *crachach. Ach y fi.*'

I couldn't believe it at first when my mother said the Morgans didn't have tuppence to put in the gas at the same time and we could easily buy them up, because although I knew the wolf was a long way from our door we seemed to live pretty close to the ground compared with them – my father came home from work dirty and never wore a gold ring on his tie, or smoked cigars like Mr. Vaughan Morgan, and we didn't have a big house like theirs either, with red tilings on the roof and a white flagstaff on the lawn. Although, when I thought about it, I saw it was true their place was battered about by the children, and whenever you went there you might find a bucket on the piano and perhaps nearly break your neck with the holes in the carpets. And upstairs you would see the marks of running water in streaks down all the bedroom wallpaper, from the winter the Vaughan Morgans had a big hole in the roof where the gutters joined, and they tied a zinc bath with ropes to the rafters to catch the rain coming in through it. Because when the bath was full, and Cuckoo and his father went up the manhole to fetch it down, they upset it between them in getting it off the ropes, and the bathful of water poured in gallons through all the ceilings and down the bedroom walls.

And once my father came in from practice laughing, saying he had just met Tommy White-hat and then acting what had happened for my mother, exaggerating everything as he always did. Mr. Vaughan Morgan had seemed as gay as usual when they had met, but when my father asked him how Annie was he changed altogether and looked very downhearted. His blue eyes filled up with tears, and he could hardly speak as he said he had just come from the hospital, where they told him she had coughed up one of her lungs that very morning, poor girl. Likely enough she had coughed up the other one by now he said, throwing away his cigar and taking his bandanna out of his breast pocket to mop his eyes with. He spoke for a long time, crying salt and describing how all his life he had lived under the showers, and how Annie had been his only comfort, so no wonder he was shedding the tears nearest his heart. My father sympathized with him and invited him down to our house for a meal of food. He thanked my father again and again for this with his hand on his shoulder, and wiping his eyes and shaking hands, he said, 'Thank you, Rhys, for your kindness in my trouble. Poor Annie, poor girl. How she's suffered – years and years of it. Nobody knows.' Here he gave a deep sigh and a final blow to his nose, and putting his spotted handkerchief away took out his gold half-hunter. 'I don't think I'll come down to-day, Rhys, my boy,' he said, 'if you don't mind. Thank you all the same. You see, I must hurry off to catch the special – I want to see the final between the Wanderers and the Thursdays.' My father watched him swaggering down the road with his white hat on the side of his head lighting another cigar.

'The dirt,' said my mother. 'No *dal* on the White-hat.'

But Arthur was always distant with people, he wasn't much like his father, friends with everybody, except that he was handsome too, and always wore smart clothes, with a bit of handkerchief showing at his breast pocket. (I noticed his nice suits because my mother used to try to make my school clothes herself, until I refused to wear them after she put the two sleeves of my jacket in backwards so that I looked like a cripple.) He was a tall slim boy with black wavy hair, pale skin and red lips, and a habit of lowering his long-lashed lids over his eyes when he was talking to you. His dog was a classy-looking bull terrier, shapely and milk-white, called Tiger, and when he saw me and my roses he winked his pink eyes and wagged his tail in an indifferent way. He was a dog who had fits and didn't seem quite right in the head by the way he behaved off the lead. Everybody hated him except the Vaughan Morgans, and once or twice they had found him laid out flat in the gutter a long way from home.

Arthur's house was in a row of big villas, where the people lived on bloaters and were in debt. We squeezed in through the swollen door that had a bulged knob, a broken fanlight, and a panel the dog had scratched into a hole with his claws, and went through to the large sunny dining-room overlooking the lawn at the back. Here Arthur left me, saying he wouldn't be long, and went upstairs with Tiger to look for Mr. Vaughan Morgan.

In this big bare room, where the shabby ceiling paper hung down at the corners like the flaps of a huge envelope, Nicholas y Glo, one of the lodgers, was sitting on a broken-backed chair reading the paper, and eating his breakfast off dishes that were all of different colours, sizes and designs. He had a bad stomach and before him, holding up the newspaper on a bit of table-cloth, were a lot of medicines – some peppermint ovals, a cup of bicarbonate of soda, and a bottle of wind and water pills. I said good morning to him, lifting a heap of washing on to the sewing machine so that I could get into the armchair, which had a hollow arm and all its springs on the floor. As I sat there carefully, with the championship roses across my knees, I noticed on the table the blue sugar-bag, and the loaf started at both ends as usual, and the tin alarm clock ticking upside down on the sideboard, and the crack in the big mirror that Mostyn,

Arthur's younger brother, had made in walking across the mantelpiece with the coal hammer in his hand. And on the wall below the American clock, whose pendulum and workings had all fallen into the glass case at the bottom, were a lot of drawings of actresses in pencil, and the huge purplish splash caused by the black-currant wine bottles exploding against the wallpaper four or five Christmases ago.

The sun's rays were pouring in so strongly upon Nicholas's waxy little head that it glistened under his thin hair, and the yellow skin looked wet, as though it had started melting. 'Good morning,' he said to me, and then he became so bashful he blushed and started whistling the bass part of the 'Men of Harlech' to himself. One reason he never said much was that he had a high falsetto voice coming out through his nose, so that whenever he spoke he sounded as though he was trying to imitate somebody. He was very nervous and he always acted queer when there were visitors about, cracking his fingers and playing with his watch-chains and tapping the table with the dishes. He was as flustered now as a fly caught in a glass of water because he knew I was watching him, and in his embarrassment he picked up his silver serviette ring and screwed it into his right eye, staring round at the cobwebs and the ceiling flies through the hole with a deep blush on his face.

But I didn't take much notice of him, my mother said he was never the same after he fell through the cellar trapdoor outside the Ship and Castle. All the boys thought him a bit queer because if there was a window rattling in chapel, or the sunset was disturbing the preacher, he would pull off his boots, blushing like a girl, and creep about the gallery in his black stockings, full of big holes, to fasten the catch or close the curtains, the joints of his feet giving off loud snaps on the floorboards at every step. He was a very tall thin man with legs like whips, wearing a black coat and striped trousers, a cream flannel waistcoat with a bunch of gold chains across it, and a very high white collar which looked as though he had stepped into it and slid it up his body into its position under his head. He had a small square face, very thin and wrinkled, and all the time he was whistling and beating on the table with his alphabet plate, and glaring at the newspaper like a one-eyed spider, I was afraid that if his jawbone lost contact with the top edge of the massive collar on which it was supported, his whole head would disappear inside, and perhaps shave off his gristly ears as it did so. The moustache on his long upper lip was perfect, neatly trimmed and waxed out, but minute, a tiny coloured model, hardly visible at all in the shadow of his nose, and yet perfect in every detail, like a tiny grub or a fly seen under a microscope. His hair was long and dry-looking, but not very plentiful, it was pressed lifeless and wiglike on to the wax of his bony scalp. But it wasn't its shape or its texture that used to attract my attention, but its colour, because it was a deep and sombre green.

There was always a lot of noise in Arthur's house, people were always coming in and out of rooms, and banging doors and shouting, and all the time I watched Mr. Nicholas as he squirmed and blushed on his broken-backed chair that creaked like an unoiled ratchet at every move, I could hear the bump-bumping noise from the other side of the wall that Mostyn was making, riding round the drawing-room on his bike. Then someone started pounding on the piano, and one of Arthur's sisters thundered up the stairs two at a time shouting out to stop it, and a fierce argument started on the landing with 'By Babylon's Wave' coming louder and louder out of the piano all the time. I hoped neither of the elder girls would burst into the dining-room and catch me with my flowers because they were very smart and witty. They had always heard of everything before and they used to use French words, like *blasé* and *à la mode*, that I wasn't sure of the meaning of.

At last there was a deafening crash as the hallstand fell over in the passage and Mostyn came skirmishing into the room fighting with Tiger.

'Hullo, Williams,' he said, staring hard at my flowers, and I only said, 'Hullo, Cuckoo,' because I didn't want to see him.

He had yellow curls and blue eyes like a girl, but he was dirty and objectionable, always smashing things and getting into a mess, and Arthur ignored him, he didn't like him at all. If one of the masters at school said, 'Arthur, is your brother present this morning?' he would answer, 'I don't know, I'll find out for you if you wish me to.' And if we happened to pass Mostyn on the other side of the street, perhaps with his thumb to his nose on the top of a lamp-post, or showing off on his yellow racer, and I said, 'Arthur, there's Cuckoo over there,' he would reply, 'I've seen him before,' without troubling to look across. And when we had passed him, he would start quoting dirty Latin.

Mostyn started pulling Tiger across the room by the ears, and then tried to get him to jump on to the table, where he knelt with his knee in the butter. He was giggling all the time and whispering something to the dog about my roses, and I could feel myself colouring because of it. He was always a nuisance, doing silly things that made Arthur sneer at him, like putting a handful of the black beetles that were always running about the house into Nicholas's cup of tea, or tying Crumpy's front door-knocker to the lamp-post. And he was the boy with a face like an angel who had five rulers stuck down his neck as soon as the master left the classroom, and his shirt pulled up over his belly and a tin box of instruments pushed into the front of his trousers.

'That will keep, Cuckoo,' I said, showing him I had heard.

At that Mr. Nicholas's blush became so plentiful it looked as though it would pass into his hair and collar and dye those scarlet too. And in his embarrassment he screwed Mr. Morgan's serviette ring into his other eye and glared hard at the newspaper before him like a goggle-eyed insect, bending his fingers so far back I was afraid they would snap off and squirt blood at the knuckles. But he was too nervous to say anything and Mostyn only laughed.

For a bit there was complete silence in the house, and in the quiet I heard the tin alarm clock stop, change gear and then begin ticking again with a deeper and more important note

But the noises started almost at once. There were two heavy bumps right above us like a couple of people falling out of bed, and in a moment or two Mr. Vaughan Morgan came into the room with a gale behind him, rubbing his gold-ringed hands and lowering the full skin-bags of his lids over his deep blue eyes against the sunglare.

'Hullo, hullo, hullo,' he said smiling, the glitter of his rings and his golden corner teeth bright like brass in the sunshine. 'Your father's roses, Evan?' he said. 'How is the old pilgrim? Don't move, my boy.' Without asking he took a little folding cigar cutter from his waistcoat pocket, snipped off the best bud he could see and put the crimson flower in his button-hole. His skin looked fresh, as though he had just come from the bath; he was wearing a pale pair of spats, a thin light grey suit with sharp creases down his trousers, and a spotted bow-tie round his wing collar. His handsome face was as pink as lint, it was clean-looking and faintly powdered after shaving, and there was some sweet-smelling oil rubbed into his thick grey hair.

He went round the table patting Nicholas on the back and putting a thin cigar out beside his plate. 'How do you feel to-day, Nat?' he said to him.

'Common,' said Mr. Nicholas in a falsetto voice like the sound squeezed out of a conjurer's dummy. The sun shone bright as a burning glass on the green back of his head, and on his collar swelling out and narrowing as he gulped his bicarbonate of soda, as though someone were pumping air through it. Then, feeling embarrassed, he got up and stood reading the newspaper before the huge marble fireplace and the cracked mirror, his big ears burning scarlet like a pair of cart-lamps hung one each side of his head. Mr. Vaughan Morgan was tall but Mr. Nicholas was taller. When I glanced at him standing there on the hearthrug, long and narrow as a vinegar-drinker, the flushes all the time coming up out of his collar and disappearing into his green hair, I thought he had his boots on the wrong feet, but when I looked again I saw his long legs were crossed behind the paper.

Everybody knew that being in the same room as Tommy Vaughan Morgan was like living at the foot of the waterfall because he could talk by the hour. His bass voice was rich and resonant, he seemed to have three or four throats when he was speaking, with a deep note bubbling out of each of them, making his voice into a harmony like a handful of keys sounded together on an organ.

'What are you trying to do, Mostyn?' he asked, ruffling Cuckoo's curls. But Cuckoo, still trying to get the dog to jump on to the table, pushed his hand away – although he was from the bottom of the nest he was always cheeky to his father. 'Like this look,' Mr. Morgan went on. He got up from the table and began calling the bull-terrier to entice him towards the casement window; this he managed to open after a lot of tugging, which made the handle come off in his hand. (It was through this window that I once saw him throwing out the dinner when Mrs. Morgan was alive. Arthur and I were below, near the flagstaff on the lawn, when we saw Mr. Morgan through the open window coming into the dining-room. He had been at the Bull, potting, by the look of him, because his white felt was low down on his ears like a comedian's bowler, his pincenez were hanging out of his waistcoat pocket and his face was sulky and flushed purple. 'Annie,' we heard him shout in his high-class way, 'what's for dinner to-day?' Arthur's mother was a quiet little woman always pattering about the house in silence, she never went out except to meet the trains in when Tommy had been away. 'Ham, my love,' she said meekly, holding before him a dish with a big lump of boiled ham on it. 'Damn the ham,' said Tommy, and he threw the meat out of the window. 'My father,' said Arthur, 'under the influence of words or liquor, exhibits a strange vehemence of behaviour.')

Tommy began fondling the dog, and when he had got him near the window he shouted, 'Cats, Tiger! Cats!' The dog gave a growl and with a clever spring disappeared through the open window and landed on the lawn outside, but when he found he had been fooled he dived with one leap back into the room again. Tommy laughed and, taking the bread-saw off the table, started to comb him with it.

'This is the most wonderful dog in the valley, Evan,' he went on, going over to the sideboard that had a row of cigar burns along the edge. 'Now where are those snaps of him, Mostyn?' He took the cigar from the table and Mostyn lit it for him with a match. With his spring pincenez on he began searching about first in the bulgy tea caddy and then in the shallow drawers, piling the contents on to the table, a dog's bone, a gym shoe, some gas mantle cases, two or three pigeon rings, a mass of clockwork, a toffee hammer, and a cigar-box holding a wad of letters and a handful of watch-wheels. He couldn't find the photographs but among the letters was a telegram which he handed to me. 'Read that, Evan,' he said. 'From our Arthur when he matriculated.' (There was one word in the telegram – *Undergraduate.*) 'This is what I was going to say. You know Mam Evans, Evan?'

'My mother's washerwoman,' I said, and Mr. Nicholas put his newspaper behind him to listen.

'On the tramroad yesterday,' he went on, 'I saw her with Sian her mother sitting in a pair of chairs outside their house. I got my watch ready because she always wants to know the time. And it's a trick to tell her the time, you know. Have you tried it, Evan?'

'Stick to your story, Tommy,' said Mostyn.

Mr. Morgan laughed. 'Mostyn *bach*,' he said pulling at his cigar. 'The lamb teaching the sheep to graze.' Then he began again, imitating the impediment of the old woman. 'If ever she asks you, tell her to the nearest quarter of an hour – she's got no looks on minutes. "Thomas Vaughan," she says to me. "Thomas Vaughan, have you got the right time, please?" So I take out my watch to tell her.'

Here Mr. Morgan opened his half-hunter, but the belly fell out on the table. He pushed it back in again and stared at it down the side of his pink Roman nose, but before he could say anything Mr. Nicholas made his middle finger go off snap behind his back with a crack like a pistol shot. Tommy was startled by the noise, and Nicholas went red and looked as though he would like to fold the big flaps of his ears over his face to hide his blushes, but he didn't dare open his beak. Then as he was getting behind the paper again, Arthur came into the room and motioned me out. I got off the armchair which gave out a long chorus of pings, like a number of tuning-forks struck in a cluster as the springs worked up one by one through the plush again, and Mr. Morgan recovered himself at the noise.

' "Well, Mam Evans," I say,' he went on, mocking the way she said s and r, ' "it's now precisely eleven minutes past five." That won't do for her at all. Not at all. "Eleven minutes past five, indeed," she says, rubbing that old scab on her chin. "What sort of time is that? Tell us the right time now, boy." I don't know what in the world to tell her, so I say, "Well, I *have* told you the right time, Mam Evans, it's now nearly twelve minutes past five." – "There's funny you are getting, Thomas Vaughan," she complains, disgusted with me, "tell us the right time now tidy and don't be so dull, boy." We go on like this until it's quarter past, and then she's satisfied.'

Tommy was in a *hwyl* by now with a story to act and an audience to listen, his blue eyes were glittering like stars and his mouth was full of spit. When he was like this he seemed overflowing with energy, and I had seen him posting a letter in the middle of a tale as though he was going to stuff his arm up to the elbow into the pillar box, and turning the kitchen tap on so that the word COLD went round and round and the water splashed all over the kitchen.

Slowly I edged round to the door, Tommy talking like the pit of the sea, telling us how the old women had hobbled out of the house frightened because Tiger had come in and was lying fast asleep by the fire in the kitchen. I stumbled over the hymn-book holding up the leg of the table, but at last I stood by Arthur near the door, ready to slip out. Before us in the liquidy sunshine of the room I could see the others as though they were in a play, Mostyn smoothing the dog with the match-

box, Tommy pink with acting his story, a trellis of lines clear
on the soft bags under his blue eyes, and Nicholas y Glo in an
upright coil on the mat, his hair green as seaweed and his
collar like a white legging rising above the paper.

And then our chance came, because we saw Mostyn setting
fire with a match to the bottom edge of the paper Nicholas was
again holding spread out before him. The sheets kindled at
once, they flared up like celluloid, divided into two by the
flames, and when Nicholas saw he held a blazing mass in each
hand his face went crimson, he let out a terrified shriek in his
high-pitched voice and began waving the burning sheets around
his head so that I was afraid his hair would catch fire, he danced
up and down on the mat shouting out, 'I'm on fire, I'm on
fire! Water! Water!' loudly through his nose. Mostyn laughed,
the dog set up a howl and dived out through the window, and
Tommy stopped with his cigar up, his golden fangs and the flat
band on his finger flashing like signals in the sun.

Arthur and I bolted out into the passage, but as we were
coming on to the path through the front door it stuck fast, and
Arthur slammed it after him with such a bang that six feet of
iron down-pipe dropped off the wall and nearly knocked me cold.

When we got to the end of the road Tiger was waiting for us,
wagging his tail and blinking.

As soon as we got back on to the tramroad we met Benja
Bowen on his way home. It was a Tuesday in the holidays, but
he said he had been to chapel. I didn't feel much like taking
him to my Uncle Sam's house because he was such a clown and
you couldn't trust him. (Once when he came with me to my
Mamgu Williams's he tried to creep into her sleeve by showing
her a balancing trick with some of her cut-glass tumblers, and
he smashed them all.) But he said, 'Going towards up?' and
when we told him we were he said he would be with us as soon
as he had changed his clothes. I couldn't think of anything to

say to stop him so we went back with him to his father's shop.

Benja was a bit mis-shapen, he was short, thick-set and bull-necked, with arms hanging down to his knees like an ape. His short powerful legs were rather bandy because he had broken both of them, and he had a great wrinkled cone of ginger hair piled up on top of his huge head like stiff coco-nut matting. His bottom jaw, covered with blond unshaved cub-fur, stuck out beyond his top and his cheeks were red, but if you called him Rosie or Cochyn he would punch you on the muscles. He had his best clothes on, an Eton collar, a black coat and vest and striped trousers stinking of tobacco, and a pair of button boots that someone had ordered from his father and never called for. His father was a bootmaker, and you could always see the top of him showing above the green-painted window of their shop, his bald head very shiny and dirty as though he had polished it a bit with the heel-ball. He was an evangelist too, and you had to keep your hat straight when you were talking to him. One night, at the time we used to live near them, my mother called round at his house to look for our groceries and when he said they hadn't been left there, my mother thought he was teasing and said, 'Go on, Mr. Bowen, aren't they here indeed?' – 'Mrs. Williams,' said Benja's father, 'my yea is yea, and my nay is nay,' and he slammed the door in her face and bolted it. My mother said *wfft* to him, she had no looks on Bowen the bootmaker after that.

But he was very strict with his children too, and sometimes Benja would turn up to play for the school wearing his ordinary clothes and only one football boot, because that was all he had been able to smuggle out of the house. And perhaps even then he had jumped out of the upstairs window into the back-yard garden. He was stupid in school, he didn't have much under his hair except for games; once when the Welsh master asked him if his home was bi-lingual, he said, 'No, sir, by the Ship and Castle.' And on the morning the school reports came out Benja would be seen skulking in the shop doorway asking people if they had seen the postman.

We thought Benja would be quicker if we didn't go inside his house so we sat on a box in the little backyard with Tiger between us. Benja's father was a queer man, and before he tried to start his own religion he used to come to our chapel and disturb the meetings by shouting out, 'Amen,' and beating his breast and groaning when the minister mentioned Judas Iscariot. You never knew what he would do next and once, when it was nearly midnight, we heard from our house a great crash, and Mrs. Bowen ran down to my mother in a fright asking if she could come in. She said her husband had got up out of bed and suddenly started sweeping the soot out of the flues, and with a mighty heave of the brush he had pushed the back kitchen chimney over into the glass house next door.

But whatever he did himself, he always sat very tight on the tails of the children, and one Sunday at tea-time he asked Benja if he had been that afternoon to the *gymanfa ganu* rehearsal at Bethel, a chapel a couple miles up the valley. Benja said yes he had, and he enjoyed the singing too. 'Where were you sitting?' asked his father. 'Behind the clock on the gallery,' said Benja. His father landed him a stinger with his heavy stitching hand on the side of the head, and chased him with a walking-stick from the table up into the bedroom. Benja was startled out of his wits up there, hearing his father roaring about downstairs and the furniture smashing, and after a couple of hours, as he sat bewildered on the bed with a kettle boiling in his hot ear, he heard his sister at the keyhole whispering his name. 'What's all that noise down there?' he asked, 'what's happening?' – 'It's our dad,' she answered, 'he's gone mad and he's attacking the back of the piano with the hatchet.' – 'What's the matter with him?' asked Benja, 'what did he hit me across the ear like that for?' – 'There's no gallery in Bethel,' she said. 'I was there.'

But that was a long time ago when Benja used to spend the time he wasn't in chapel swimming in the canal where the hot water poured out of the boiler-house, and teasing the pawnbroker by spitting on his crossed fingers outside the shop window.

After a bit Benja came out dressed in his holiday clothes instead of his dark suit and Eton collar. He was wearing over his pile of ginger hair a man's tweed cap with the broken peak pointing skywards, and his grey suit so shrunken with boiling that the tight bandy trousers were above his boots and the cuffs almost up to the elbows of his monkey arms. And under his jacket he had a white cycling sweater tied with waxed thread round his waist to stop it hanging down to his knees like a shirt.

The three of us started out again for my uncle's with Tiger trotting behind us like a back sergeant, and as we passed the front of Benja's shop we could see the dirty top of his father's head showing above the green paint, it was bald and shining as though he had held it hard against the spinning brushes he kept for polishing the leather in the shop. We turned into the tramroad once more, just where I had met the crimson contralto, passing Dai Ben-tip nursing the baby with the shawl wrapped all round him, and M'Liza's brother, William the Rates, resting his bad leg on a window sill. He had a big black beard and hair all over him, and he growled all day long like a big dog who wants you to spit on a stone and throw it for him. As we passed by, Benja said something cheeky and the old man hit him across the behind with his walking-stick. But Benja only laughed and soon he began smoking a cigarette nip, pulling hard at it, grimacing, hollowing his ginger-haired cheeks and wrinkling up his eyes as though it was a hard job to suck any smoke out of it.

After a while he began telling us again about the time he went abroad to play for the country against the French schoolboys (his father didn't know till after, he thought he was bad with the bile in his Auntie Blod's in the next valley) and how they gave him so much brandy over there they couldn't keep him in his seat at the banquet, and before he was sick he wanted to fight the Mayor of Paris. He always made me laugh with this story, but Arthur didn't take any notice of him.

Then to annoy me and Benja, Arthur started talking about Horace and Catullus, and we didn't know anything about those poets because he had got up into a form above us now. We were sorry they had separated us because you could get fun out of the cool way Arthur always spoke to the masters, like when he cheeked Crumpy in the Latin lesson and told him of course he had a crib and he found he couldn't do without it. Besides, Benja didn't have anyone to copy off now. Benja never had much time to do his homework because he was always in chapel, or boxing over Imperato's, so he used to scribble Arthur's lessons out behind the fives court during dinnertime, fetching a pen and an inkwell stuffed with paper out of school for the job. He was always in such a hurry that he used to make a broth of it with blots and smudges, and when he had finished he used to throw the pen and the inkwell away into the bushes and hurry down town without us for a smoke and a game of billiards. (I wouldn't go with him now, because the only time I went I found a couple of yellow snooker balls in my schoolbag when I got home.)

Very soon Benja had had a bellyful of Horace and Catullus, and he started talking about the footwork of Maxy Imperato, because that was the only thing he knew more about than Arthur. I didn't much care what they talked about as long as it wasn't my bunch of roses, but presently Arthur said, 'What did you say was the matter with your uncle, Williams?'

'Asthma,' I said. 'Chronic.'

'Asthma,' he said, 'and you're taking him flowers. Don't you know things like that plastered with pollen will bring on an attack for him?'

I was angry with him and I said that was old-fashioned talk, fly-me, like spitting on warts and having a potato for rheumatism, but I knew for sure somehow he was right. I felt cross with my mother, it was just like her to do this to me. (I couldn't help remembering the time my cousins were coming for Christmas when I was small, and she gave me and Rhysie a sleeping draught to stop us getting excited. But she gave us so much we slept fast for three days and we never saw our cousins at all.)

'I've never seen anyone having an attack of asthma,' said Benja in a thoughtful way, grinning and picking at his bad teeth. So I was feeling worried when at last we got outside my uncle's house, and all I wanted to do was to get away as soon as I could.

My Uncle Sam's stone house was very small, and so full of furniture that there were only narrow passages in between the hulking dressers and the chests of drawers for you to move about in. Every shelf and flat space had big Bibles on it, or collier's lamps or crowds of photographs and china mementos, and you could hardly see the wallpaper anywhere because of the family enlargements, and the Rechabites' calendars, and the massive furniture big enough for a palace or a castle. My Auntie Maggie was very clean and always smelling of carbolic, she was for ever smoothing the table oilcloth with her apron, and using her goose's wing on the curtains, and scouring the handles of her sweeping brushes with red sand to keep them white. And though it was misty in her kitchen now, as dim as the inside of a bottle, still every piece of wood and every strip of metal shone like polished glass in the smoky gloom, especially the heavy brass airing rail, and the steel stand and fender, and the gleaming fringe of brass around the mantelpiece. My uncle and auntie always lived in this little box of a kitchen, which had a bosh in the corner smelling of soap, and white stoning swirls on the floor, and a square of drying wires on the ceiling, and a chimney that was always blowing down clouds of stife into the room in winter. They had a nice parlour too, but my auntie only used that to let the jellies set in, and whenever you walked about in there the soles of your boots stuck to the oilcloth and all the ornaments trembled.

I liked my Uncle Sam ever since I was small and he taught

me corkwork. He used to draw a flag for me then, and the
gwdihw, and harlequin, or swallow his watch on the end of a
string and let me hear it ticking in his belly. He was my
favourite uncle, although I knew he was a born liar. When he
was a young man he had run away because my Mamgu Thomas
used to beat him for buying bottle beer with the money from his
drapery round. But he was old now and bald, and a bit deaf, he
looked very respectable drowsing in the rocking chair by the
fire, with a snowy shawl round his shoulders and a jug of herb
beer in his hand. He was wearing a washed suit after my father
and a pair of old carpet slaps, and round his neck there was a
black knitted tie but no collar. And although he hadn't done a
tap for years now, you could tell it was true he had once been
working underground because there was a jagged blue mark
running like quartz across his forehead, and continuing in a
thick blue vein down his cheek. He had yellow eyeballs, a red
nose as bright as a berry and brown bamboo marks mottling
the skin of his long hanging cheeks. His moustache was small
now (when he was on his wanderings it had been a huge one
shaped like a steer's horns or the badge of the Buffs) and because
he hadn't shaved his bristling chin glittered like a stubble of
hoar-frost. He had been ailing so long he smiled with pleasure
when he saw us, showing his bad teeth under his moustache.
All my uncle's teeth were of different colours and sizes. Some
were brown, some yellow and some slatish, and one buff-
coloured tooth would be twice the height of the little black
stump standing next to it.

My Auntie Maggie made us go inside the kitchen, dog and
all, to talk to Uncle Sam. She was always dressed in baggy
black, and she was fat and soft all over, with a lap like a feather-
bed. Her face was clean and handsome, she had a lot of grey
horse-hair, a big curved nose and a lovely smile, but there was
something the matter with one of her eyes – the right ball was
fixed and pitch black, it stood bulging out of her head and
shining with the polish of the big black-leaded pebble that kept
the back door open, and it never slid about into the corners at

all. At one time, after chapel on Sunday nights, my uncle and auntie used to come down our house to sing hymns round the parlour harmonium, while my father accompanied us on the trombone. My auntie had a lovely soprano voice then but her favourite Sunday night solo was called ''Tis Heaven or Hell with you and me', and she used to frighten the life out of me with that song, because the great polished knob of her stuck eye was fixed fast upon me the whole time she was singing it, making me remember all the times I had smoked, and told lies, and even gone up the woods miching. I knew where I was going, and in the dead silence after her song, with only the globe of the gaslight ringing, I could feel my hair creeping about on my head.

But all that was years ago and I knew now my auntie was innocent, she would believe anything. And she waited on my uncle hand, foot and finger, saying, 'You'll come, come you,' to him all the time to cheer him up a bit. She was a lovely woman and she put the roses out the back where Mam Evans was getting the washing ready, without hurting my feelings, although Benja wanted to take them into the kitchen for my uncle to have a good smell.

Although I was so anxious to get away we had a tidy little time talking to my Uncle Sam. We could hear the two women banging about among the buckets outside the window behind us, my auntie using the canebrush like mad on the back, and every now and then popping the big black knob of her horse-eye up against the pane, and staring through the geranium leaves to see how we were getting on. The three of us sat in a row on the couch opposite my uncle, and he told us interesting lies with gusto about America and Woolangong and other places, but none of us believed him; we had the yarn about the man who worked in the airways, and the tale of how my uncle found that week's *Football Echo* in the middle of the Australian bush when he was a lost man out there. (Benja grinned at that, his teeth like barnacles on his gums. 'And now tell us the one about the three bears,' he said.)

At times my uncle would get so excited he would have to stop his tale for a bit of puff, or to take a swig out of his herb jug, sucking his soaking moustaches into his mouth after he had done it. 'The old bellows,' he would mutter, pointing to his chest and smiling. With the fire lit, the door closed and the sun shining hot outside, the boxy little room was becoming warmer and warmer, and I would move to go while my uncle was drinking, but Benja would say, 'Take a blow, Evan, I think he's got an attack coming on,' although he was hot in his white sweater. But nothing happened, and I would have to sit down again while my uncle hooked his hand like the skinny yellow claw of a boiling fowl around his ear, trying to catch what Benja was saying.

When we made my uncle understand who Arthur was he rolled his amber eyeballs with pleasure and laughed, shaking his hanging mottled cheeks, he knew Tommy Morgan well, and his father the Gentleman Miner before him, and he began telling stories about him when he was a young cutter, before he got his tail into the mud. Arthur smiled, very polite, hanging on to Tiger's collar, but he didn't say much, he was too indolent to shout although really he was a fine conversationalist; he used to talk very far back and use phrases you couldn't undertsand like 'the perihelion of Mercury', and 'the pucelage and virginity of women.'

But Benja didn't mind shouting and he began showing off like a red-headed ape, telling my uncle fairy tales about his family, and turning round to show the scar on the back of his ginger head that he said his mother had done when she crowned him with the frying-pan because he couldn't remember the three headings of a sermon on charity. (Arthur and I knew that really he had bolted some secondhand spring expanders up in the attic on the sly, and when he went to use them the hook had pulled out of the wood and nearly brained him.) He had started his clowning as soon as he had come in, shaking hands with my uncle and auntie with the wrong hand like a big-headed gnome, and grinning at them as though he were an idiot, the gaps in his teeth showing like book-backs missing from a shelf. He was daft now and his nonsense made me hotter than ever, although I had to laugh when he rolled up his tight trousers and showed the birthmark on his bandy leg shaped like the Caspian Sea that he said had made him top of the class when he copied it on his geography paper. 'Come on, Benja,' I said standing up, wanting to peg him back a bit because my uncle was laughing and sweating at the same time; his snowy shawl was down behind him in the bars of the rocker and he was holding his chest with his bright yellow fist, his eyes shut tight, his cheeks puffed out and his puce tongue showing under his moustache with a fit of coughing.

But before I could get him to move my auntie padded smiling and bulge-eyed into the kitchen, sidling with her tin tray among the massive mahogany, and gave us a thick slice of apple-tart each, and a fork to get it up with. Then she went over to my uncle and tidied him up a bit, wiping his ripe red nose and dusting his face with her apron as though he were a piece of furniture, persuading him to have another dose of Cough-no-more as she draped the shawl around his shoulders. Then, when we had started eating, Mam Evans came in with some of the things *she* liked, bread and cheese and a jampot of pickle cabbage which she put down on the table for us. They never had anything with vinegar in it in Benja's, because Bowen the bootmaker had found out the word meant 'sour wine', so when no one was looking Benja threw his piece of tart under the couch and started enjoying the pickle cabbage.

'Bowen,' said Arthur, 'why do you catch your fork so low down?'

I didn't notice that Benja held his fork low down, but I always used to look at his finger with the top off.

Mam Evans, who stood by the table as we were eating, dipping now and then into the pickle cabbage with a spoon and a piece of bread, had a face like rubber or fresh putty. She had no teeth, and because her mouth was right up under her nose she seemed to be chewing with her nostrils. And her flabby head with the watery blue eyes in it, and the toe-nail growing out of her chin, seemed narrow compared with her neck because on each side she had a smooth and solid wen. She was wearing a pair of clogs, her black flannel working clothes with a canvas apron round her, and a man's cap fastened with a hat-pin through her bun.

She listened to my uncle telling Arthur and Benja the old story of how he fell down and kissed the railway line in *hiraeth* when he was abroad, because he saw by the stamp on it it was rolled not fifty yards from my Mamgu's house, and then she interrupted him, chewing all over her face. 'Sam Thomas,' she said loudly, 'you won't laugh at me will you?'

My uncle stopped his story and we all looked at her.

'Laugh at you, Mam Evans?' he said, when he understood her. 'What do you mean? Laugh at you?'

'Well, if I ask you a question you won't laugh at me will you?' She had big baggy hands like coal-gloves and she played with her scabby chin.

'Of course not,' said my Uncle Sam, all his different coloured teeth showing like a street skyline. 'What do you want to know?'

'Well you've been to America abroad, haven't you?'

'Yes I have, Mam Evans,' my uncle answered, his yellow talon hung on his ear.

'And you know the sun and the moon?'

My uncle nodded, 'Yes I do, of course.'

'You won't laugh at me will you?'

'No no, I won't laugh, go on.'

'Well do they have the same sun and moon in America as we do have here?'

We all laughed at that, my uncle and all, and Benja threw his feet in their button boots into the air. My uncle said yes they had the same sun and moon, and at that Mam Evans clumped back to her work, chewing and grumbling at us and taking snuff, her skirts down at the sides and up at the back.

My auntie stood by smiling too as we were eating, landed

that we were enjoying ourselves, and then she began questioning
me about Rhysie and my mother. Anybody else would see
I didn't want to talk about our mam just then, but my auntie
was so innocent she didn't notice. Our door-knocker was a solid
brass hand with a palmed brass ball in it, and when I couldn't
hold her off any longer I had to blurt out my mother's foot was
bad because when she was going to chapel she pulled the front
door after her, and the knocker came away as she did it. She
came a cropper down our five steps and landed up with her leg
under the gate, and she had to go to chapel with the brass
knocker weighing three or four pounds in her overcoat pocket.
I was ashamed to say what had happened because everyone
would say it was just like my mother, so I ended by turning to
Benja and saying, 'Don't start on that culff, Benja, let's go
home.'

He shook his big head, his cheeks full of bread and his bad
teeth quarrying the cheese. 'Take a blow, mun,' he growled like
a prompter, 'the bloke that made time made plenty of it.'

Arthur had let go his hold on Tiger to eat his tart, and the
dog had his paws up on the couch, hoping for a bit of it.
Suddenly he growled and quivered all over, and without any
more warning jumped on to the couch alongside us, and then
bolted straight out through the window from between the
geraniums, he took a header clean through the glass as though
it wasn't there at all and disappeared out of sight. The pane
shattered into fragments, leaving only a fringe of jagged pieces
like a paper hoop around the edges, and there was the deafening clatter of an accident with trays among the buckets in the
backyard. We all jumped up and stared out of the window,
feeling the cool air at once on our faces, my uncle behind us
gripping our arms and wheezing with excitement. Arthur
began whistling through the broken pane after the dog, which
had galloped along the path and was now standing rigid near
the garden wall, on which the next door's tabby was sitting,
and gradually getting smaller in safety. 'Tiger, Tiger,' he called
coolly. 'Come here, boy. Come here, boy.' And at last Tiger

turned round and came bounding and diving back down the garden path towards the kitchen again. He saw Arthur standing by the broken glass of the window, and without any hesitation he plunged back into the room through the other pane, bursting it like a water-bubble, and bringing all the geraniums down on to the couch behind him as he tumbled over on to the mat. Arthur gripped him by the collar and began slapping him about the head, his black hair hanging in curves like the claws of a pair of callipers over his face.

My auntie, who used to pick my uncle up at the front doorstep when it was raining and battle her way through the passage with him on her back to keep the oilcloth clean, didn't know what to do, she just sat down on the stool and said, '*O wel ta wir*,' with her face in a twist and her glued eye staring at the mess on the floor. Because it was a sad sight to her, as bad as a pig's breakfast spoiling the stoning on her lovely hearth. There were pieces of glass scattered all over her spotless kitchen, and the geranium pots in falling had split open and the earth lay spread in dollops all over the hearthrug, mixed with fragments of cheese and red cabbage and flakes of pastry. And the dog, who had opened his bowels with fright on the mat when he crashed like a cannon-ball back into the room, had made my uncle fall over backwards into the rocker, overturning the little table behind him and sending all the crockery to the floor, including the Mabon milk-jug, and splashing the herb beer all over the wall and the cupboard and the black-leaded fireplace, where it ran down the oven in long tears.

Just then Mam Evans put her head on the end of her wide wenny neck around the door, a snuff stain on her nose and her bottom lip fitted up over her top like the flap of a bandage.

'Maggie Thomas,' she said, not noticing anything with her pale half-liquid eyes, 'I want a bit of soda. Have you got a bit of soda?'

But my auntie took no notice of her, she sat glaring downwards with her black ornamental eye and muttering to herself, '*O wel ta wir. O wel ta wir.*'

Suddenly, in the middle of all the mess, I noticed Benja's face. He wasn't paying any attention to my auntie, or to Mam Evans squinting round the corner, or to Arthur slapping the dog, he was gaping at my Uncle Sam's bald head starting to simmer, and his blue wound growing brilliant on his forehead, and his boiling chest beginning to bubble like a kettle as his shoulders heaved up under his ears. He sat fascinated, his short finger in his nose, his lower jaw hung out like a balcony, and a daft smile of satisfaction on his face as the attack began to develop.

THE WATER MUSIC

Shall I dive, shall I dive? Behind me the patterns of the coloured town I left lying spread out in the green valley are like a carpet taken out on the grass for beating, and I race down the sunny slope out of sight of it. I am a flier with the wind rushing under the bony arches of my wings, I am a white gull, I am two-hundred gulls, I am the gull-shower of snow in sunshine, and the whirled flakes of summer whitening the world. I turn my beaked face and out of a bright eye I see beside my head, rigid and purposeful, my crooked wing, with its piled-up foam-crest of feathers broken wave-white along its ridge in the speed-created wind; I see the few cricketing children dwarfed in the tree-surrounded meadow, and the grannie in black who minds their picnic fire, and the column of wood-smoke upright in the odorous air of the field. Beyond the curtain of foliage surrounding the oval meadow glitters the curve of the river in silver patches, poured like a flat snake among the trees, sundering the rooted feet that crowd upon its bank. And beside the river's biggest pool rises the grey diving-rock, the stone of the cliff in sunshine pale as coltsfoot leaf, but felt-smooth, and smouldering warm to the fingers. Shall I dive, shall I dive?

As I stood by the little sherbet shop at the cornfield gate and looked over the wheat, a large broken-hearted bird came crying inland on long transparent wings like knives, radiant as fine sailcloth or sunlit snow. He was a beautiful gull, and after circling he came to rest on one leg like a wine-glass upon the gate-post beside me. He had a lovely white neck, and the sun-kindled curve of his swelling breast gleamed white as the milky dazzle of coconut kernel in the sunshine which he faced. Over his powerful boxer's back was spread a mantle of smooth dove-grey feathers, and below the glitter of his theatrically darkened eye-disc he had a brilliant broom-yellow bill, long, curved and tigerish, with a blob of blood-orange red painted near the nostrils.

'Gull,' I said in bad Latin, 'why have you left your green egg?' – 'Wha, wha, wha,' was his reply, as he folded up his webs and flew off rapidly up the valley ahead of me. Shall I dive?

Now I am across the scented meadow and through the partition of trees, I climb the high grey diving-rock and see the bathers undressing on the cliff-shelves opposite, or already swimming in pure water. I greet twenty boys from my crocketed pinnacle, waving towel and black triangular slip, hailing red-tied Thomas as comrade, a ginger boy with freckles and the blue eyes of a black kitten as neighbour Williams, and having to cry 'Gracias' to the pale and orphaned Scabbo Ball, who, wishing me well, addresses me with a bow as señor. The water beneath is limpid, the pebbles and the sandy bottom waver under it, smoothly it flows over them like flawed glass. Shall I dive with the speed of the gull, or like the capering swallow who plunges with shut wings?

Below me among the rocks is the perfectly fitting pool, large and circular, with the sun shattered upon its surface; there is the voluminous river cataracting down the grey limestone steps, in crystal fans and ferns and luminous ice-sheets, and floods of clear rock-varnish, and bunches of glass bananas; there at the far end is the dim tunnel that receives the sliding river in a long sealskin volute out of the dazzling floor of the pool; the down-drench of birch-boughs, and the green masses of beech-leaves sleek under the smooth glove of the sunshine, are arched over the glossy water. A broad scarlet towel-stripe glows unbearable as ruby on the grey rock, the black-slipped boys in naked groups lounge white and delicate in midday moon-flesh, and warm, on the sunlit shelves of the little cliff. Rosie Bowen the bootmaker's boy, begotten of mild mother and boxing-glove-burning sire, ignoramus, *victor ludorum*, stands in the water severed at the knees, with half-revealed distaste upon a dunce's countenance of endearing and transcendental ugliness. As he ponders somebody throws a pebble into the water, and his back is splashed.

'Ay Scabbo,' he shouts without looking round. 'I'll dig you in the chin.'

And then he slowly advances over the velvet-growing stones like a thief among snares or a sufferer from foot-warts; with the pool-water chilling his bandy legs he is hesitant as Dic Dywyll, reluctant and maladroit now, no reckless Christmas morning plunger to be met with, an ice-hammer in his pocket, on the track to the frozen tarn. He toes the slippery pool-stones in his path, each bearded with a long phlegm of green weed, into water as clear as crystal he peers with the intensity of a louse-hunting mother examining the hair of her dirtiest. By spreading to the sun his boxer's ape-arms, powerful and muscular under their gleaming ginger fell, he achieves for a moment the unstable balance of the tight-rope artiste. He is an indifferent concealer of his dislike of this element in its icy mountain freshness, unwarmed by equatorial current or outpoured boiler-water from the pit-head engine-room; but gradually he sinks into the depths of the pool, the blackish Caspian birthmark on his leg is submerged, the rings spread from his hairy thighs and, finding with his soles a rock-slab in the river bed when the water is around his waist, he crosses his arms in respite on his chest, and tucks into his armpits his yellow iron-mould hands – because he would smoke tea-leaves, or sea-weed, or even indiarubber. His abnormal homeliness in the pool is as rare as great villainy or genius. Upon his giant head is sewn a dense fibrous hump of coco-nut hair; his cheeks even now are tomato-red, and his protrusive lower jawbone with the liquorice stumps of disordered black teeth, gapes open like a half-shut bottom drawer. Were I to dive and come up beside him, before punching he would stare with the incredulity of Gerallt's soldier voiding a calf. Dare I dive into this huge water?

Under a tree with the curving tail of a branch hanging down over the water stands Arthur Vaughan Morgan, Rosie's friend, tall and lovely-limbed, forgetting now the humiliation of battered tea-spoons, and the charred cork for a knob in the broken teapot lid; he leans garlanded and naked in a dance-dress of sunlight flimsily patterned with transparent foliage. And Evan Williams, the third of The Three, his hair corrugated like biscuit-paper, surreptitiously unrobes behind a jut of rock, concealing thus the unique and resourceful fastenings of his broken underwear. He removes last a sort of check bodice with a frilled waistline. He has orange-golden hair and orange-golden freckles you couldn't put a pin between. He does not wear the black school bathing triangle but a scalene slip of his own devising, fashioned from a pair of bootlaces and a folded red handkerchief covered with white polka dots. That Sterne-visaged grammarian, our English master, who annihilates me with sarcasm when I audibly praise heaven for prose-writers who use two words where one will do, yet reads aloud with approval to the assembled form my essay upon the virtues of our native land. 'Glory be to the Isle of the Mighty for her ponds and the pools of all her rivers,' he sneers, 'for Pwll Wat, and Pwll Tâf, and Pwll Tydfil. And for her lakes, for Llangorse and Llyn y Fan, and for Llyn Safaddon lovely under Dafydd's swan.'

'Let there be praise also for the pools of the Po and for the waters of Lake Titicaca,' Evan whispers behind my blushing ear.

'Praise her for her towns and villages and her ancient divisions, praise her for Gwynedd and Powys and Dyfed and Morgannwg. Praise her for her lovely names, for Llanrhidian, Afon Sawdde, Fan Girhirych, Dyffryn Clwyd. Praise her for Rhosllanerchrugog——'

'And for Llanfairpwllgwyngyllgogerychwyrndrobwllllandy-siliogogogoch,' softly intones Williams to a mutilated version of 'Hen Wlad fy Nhadau'.

'Let us praise her for Llŷn and Llanelli, for Dinas Mawddwy and Dinas Powis, for Cwm Elan and Cwm Rhondda, let us praise Tresaith equally with Treorky and Penrhyn Gŵyr equally with Pengarnddu.'

'Let us praise Moscow equally with Little Moscow,' growls Evan, 'and Llantwit Major equally with Asia Minor,' and the only thing to do is to cough.

Now Bolo Jones the overman's boy, togaed in many towels, wishing to show Arthur little Dai Badger denounced as Catiline and indignantly interrogated as to when he shall cease oppressing the people, shouts down, 'Acker, Acker, look at this.'

Arthur, dappled under his hanging bough, ignores him.

'Acker Morgan,' shouts undaunted Bolo again from his proscenium, a grey ledge of rock six feet above the water, his arm outstretched in indignation towards the singing Catiline.

Arthur frowns, examining his nails. He is a cock with a high comb. His three sisters are knowing and fashionable, they have haughty expressions but short legs.

'Ack – er,' shouts Bolo once more, loud above the cries and the chorus singing and the low roar of the river rushing into the pool with the splash of water washing itself all over.

Arthur turns towards him. 'My name is Arthur,' he says testily. 'Arthur – heroic and European. Arthur Trevelyan Vaughan Morgan.'

Bolo Jones drops his towels, claps his hand to his head and collapses backwards into the pool.

And dare I dive from this height into the water?

Rosie Bowen is swimming. He has waded up to the foot of the cataract now and, using a breast-stroke, proceeds kicking with the help of the current down the middle of the water. His swimming is laborious and convulsive, like a frog who has swallowed a handful of lead-shot, but everyone remembers Imperato's and his head is not pushed under. On the lowest ledge of the cliff opposite, Phil and Sinky swing a grinning Dai Badger to and fro by the wrists and ankles, while Scabbo, his body white as pipe-clay, gives them his orders. 'Away with him,' he cries, 'cast the perjured caitiff into the roaring torrent of the river.' – 'The traitor says he cannot swim, my lord,' says Sinky. 'Clearly,' answers Scabbo, 'here's a fine chance for him to learn.' Dai bounds outwards, he enters the water in the button of a ragged bloom of spray. Bleddyn Beavan, who has just climbed out to watch, bends smiling in a sleek skin with his toes gripping the rock brink, his hands on his knees and a thread of water running back into the pool off his chin. All of us in our form have a firm and scientifically accurate knowledge of our physical genesis, because his father is Doctor Gomer and Bleddyn will lend you his medical books at tuppence a week. Shall I dive?

When I was small and dirty, with a quilted bottom to my trousers, I wanted only to learn swimming. Out of my big brother's book I spelled this sentence: 'The action of the frog should be studied and imitated.' On washing day I miched and went up Cwm Ffrwd, croaking about by the river like a frog. At last I found a big green one weighing a quarter of a pound. I put him in my cap to bring him home and he didn't like that because my cat used to sleep in it every night. My mother had two tubs of clothes-water in our back and I put him in the one for the flannels. I made him swim about in the warm water among the shirts and the nightgowns, and soon I could swim lovely. When I heard my mother coming I put him down the lavatory and poured a bucket of water on top of him.

That evening I went up the pit-pond on the tips where the collier-boys used to swim dirty. I climbed on to the timber balks and dived in. When I woke up a big crowd of men was carrying me home across the fields on a stretcher. I thought I had been punished for drowning the frog who had taught me to swim. At home the doctor said, 'And last week he pulled the coping of the Methodist Chapel wall down on his chest.'

The same summer my mother took us to the Wells for our holidays. I borrowed tuppence off my brother and went for a swim in the open-air baths. I had never been to a baths before. The water was black and crowded with people. I dived in at the shallow end. This time when I came to I was stretched out on the mohair couch in our lodgings, with my skin cold as glass and a big smooth lump like a tea-cup on the front of my head.

And now dare I dive?

Behind me, across the meadow, I see through the trees the luminous green slope where I was a rugger-running gull, tilted to the sunglare, the grass seething in the summer sunbeams, vivid and crystalline, the brightness glowing over the kindled surface with a teeming lustre of intense emerald, as though the grassy fabric were a sheet of transparent crystal evenly illuminated with rays of pure greenish fire from beneath. And over it goes my gull, rigid and ravenous, crying, 'Wah, wah, wah.' He is beautiful enough to be addressed by the wandering scholar who said, 'Lovely gull, snow-white and moon-white, immaculate sun-patch and sea-glove, swift-proud fish-eater, let us fly off hand-in-hand, you are light on the waves as a sea-lily. My grey nun among sea-crests, you shall be my glossy letter, go and carry a *billet* to my girl for me and win distant praise by making for her fortress. You shall see her, Eigr-coloured, on her castle, gull. Carry her my note, my chosen, go girl-wards. If she is alone, do not be shy of talking to her, but be tactful in the presence of so much fastidiousness. Tell her I shall die without her, and look, gull, tell her I am over head and ears in love with her, that not even Merddin or Taliesin desired her superior in beauty. Gull, under her tangled crop of copper you shall behold Christendom's loveliest lovely – but she'll be the death of me if you bring no for an answer.'

'Take my boots off when I die, when I die,' sings Dai Badger, shaped like a ship's anchor floating on the surface of the pool.

'Take my boots off when I die.'

The butcher's cart and bill-heads of Dai's father bear the slogan, 'Let Badger be your Butcher,' which seven-syllabled line, in the opinion of that erratic but pithy critic Evan Williams, contains more poetry and *cynghanedd* than the similarly horta-tory but more famous words of the High Priest of Lakery urging us to take Nature for our Teacher. For Evan, who always hears of such things, has solved the riddle of Hamlet. The clue lies, he maintains, with the hidden character called Pat, addressed directly only once, and that in the tortured reflection of young Denmark – 'Now might I do it, Pat, now he is praying,' but whose machinations and subtle influence have confounded three hundred years of criticism. Shall I dive now like a glider of the boughs?

Dai Badger is again on the shelf, juicy-nosed, counting his tail-feathers after his ducking and the bravado of his song. He spots me watching him across the pool and wants to know if I will come over the mountain with him to-morrow. 'To where?' I ask cautiously. 'One A one b one e one r one d one a one r one e,' he cries at breathless speed. 'Will you?' He is a fabulist and claims to be in love with the vicar's Swiss maid there, who is indeed a nicely shaped young woman but twice his size. I make an excuse and he sings a wicked ballad describing his passion for her foreign body. He feels no *pudeur* at our natural out-curves and tuberosities and his naked belly now is tight as a bagpipe with lyricism. But Rosie Bowen, hearing him, spits into the water; he has coco-nut hair, an undershot jaw and, to a god's-eye view, a hump like a high bosom on his back; he spits copiously and without displaying muscular action, projecting a large and heavy gob downstream without a twitch of his face, sending it flying in a sweet curve from his immobile face.

And now shall I dive?

Arthur leaves the shelter of his tail-shaped tree and stands among the swimmers on the soaking ledge, like a patrician candidate heroically facing the malodorous citizens. Flicker, our mathematics master, who declares so-and-so to be an outstanding this, that and the other, if he would only more frequently 'duck his nut', is despised by Arthur, the inelegant phrasing, bad breath and linoleum waistcoat of this unpleasant sciolist deeply offend him. 'Here is a clever chap,' sneers Flicker, distributing the marked examination papers after his terminal test, 'Arthur Morgan, the famous mathematical genius. He can solve a quadratic equation in one line! Stand up Morgan! You cooked the answer!'

'I didn't,' says Arthur with dignity.

'You did,' shouts Flicker, reddening and bulge-eyed.

'I didn't,' says Arthur.

'You did,' shouts Flicker.

'Oh, all right,' says Arthur sitting down. 'I'll give you the benefit of the doubt.'

But he is teased because Bolo Jones has his photograph taken in his first long-trousered sailor-suit, with a cane whistle on a cord and a fouled anchor worked on his front.

Below me where the water is quiet, foam in clusters of pappus, and pints of cuckoo-spit, and fine meshes of foam thin as beer-froth, float on the dark water; under the overhanging boughs of the boy-bodied beeches and the cataracting birches, a broken mesh of reflected gold is thrown up in the gloom, the network of uneasy golden light on the under-branches is torn apart, and joined up again, as the green liquid glass of the water is splashed and the sunlight scattered. A breeze starts, the wind is handed on from tree to tree. I hear near me the first soft clatter of the poplar leaves. Soon the swimming will be over and I dawdle and have not dived. Rosie retires shivering in the hot sunshine, cold beyond the reach of wine or smith's fire. Evan says a swig would be welcome as hail in hell and Dai Badger shouts, 'I feel poppish too.' They dress and leave to-gether for the widow's shop at the cornfield gate where, on a piece of torn cardboard, for the information of picnickers, is chalked the message – 'Hot water sold here. Pop round the corner.' I must dive.

Shooting down the silky chasm of my plunge, with my soles to the brilliant county blue and the cortex of that highly convolved and dazzling cloud, I shall be the gull off her olive egg, the diving gull from the dovey dawn, the herring-gull or blackback falling like large snow off the roof of the world. Rosie is a powerful land-animal, Evan charming and un-awakened, Arthur learned in Latin, beautiful as Sande or some musk-scented princess; but I am the finest swimmer in this water and the only person who knows what a *vidame* is. My lungs are full, with hirundine screamings I hurdle hedges, I plunge performing the devil-dive of a star. I bomb the water blind and all images are shattered in my head. I sink and soon it is silent there, the dark beards of the stones wave as though in the breeze, and the small grains of sand bowl in the current along the bottom of the pool. My breath rises like anchor-bubbles through water green as glass edges, I lie deep like sand-eel, water-snake, or Welsh Shelley under the ten-foot slab of transparent green, watching it reach the world of my God whom I continue to praise, whom I praise for the waters, the little balls of dew and the great wave shooting out its tassel; I praise him for the big boy-bodied beeches, and all trees velvet in sunshine and shying like mad when the grass is flat under the wind; I praise him for the blooms of the horned lilac, for the blossomed hawthorn with the thick milks of spring rising over her, and the blood-drop of the ladybird bled on the white lily. I praise him for the curving gull, the brown coat of the sparrow and the plover with wings like blown hair.

I praise him for words and sentences, I praise him for Flicker Wilkins and for Arthur Vaughan Morgan and his sisters in fashionable hats like low buckets; I praise him for Bolo Jones and Dai Badger and Scabbo Ball, and for Scabbo Ball's auntie who keeps the public weighing machine and has green glasses and one hand. I praise him for the golden freckles of Evan Williams as much as for Rosie Bowen who suffers a traumatic malforma-tion of the jaw.

I praise him for the things for which I have not praised him and for the things praised only in the pleats of my meaning.

I praise him for his endless fertility and inventiveness, that he stripes, shades, patches and stipples every surface of his creation in his inexhaustible designing, leaves no stretch of water unmarked, no sand or snow-plain without the relief of interfering stripe, shadow or cross-hatch, no spread of pure sky but he deepens it from the pallor of its edges to its vivid zenith. I praise him that he is never baulked, never sterile, never repetitious.

There is praise for him in my heart and in my flesh pulled over my heart, there is praise for him in my pain and in my enjoying. I show my praise for him in the unnecessary skip of my walk, in my excessive and delighted staring, in the exu-berance of my over-praise.

And when I dive I shall feel the ice of speed and praise him, the shock and tingle of the gold-laced pool and praise him, the chrism of golden sunshine poured on my drenching head again and praise him.

I dive into the engulfing water praising him.

JORDAN

I am worried. Today when I cut my chin with my white-handled razor I didn't bleed. That was the way Danny's shaving went. Danny was my friend. Together we had a spell working the fairs and markets out there in that country where there are nothing but farms and chapels. It was a sort of un-civilized place. I had invented a good line, a special cube guaranteed to keep the flies off the meat, and Danny had his little round boxes of toothpaste. This toothpaste he scraped off a big lump of wet batter, a few pounds of it, greenish in colour and with a bad smell, it stood on a tin plate and sometimes Danny would sell it as corn cure. So as to gather a crowd around his trestle he used to strip down to his black tights and walk about with a fifty-six pound solid iron weight hanging by a short strap from his teeth. This was to show what wonderful teeth you would have if you used Danny's toothpaste. It was only when he was doing this that you ever saw any colour in Danny's face. The colour came because he did the walking about upside down, he was on his hands doing it with his black stockings in the air.

Danny was thin and undersized. If I made a joke about his skinny legs he would lower his lids offended and say, 'Don't be so personal.' He was very touchy. His tights were coms dyed black and they looked half empty, as though large slices had been cut off from inside them. He had a fine, half-starved face, very thin and leathery, like a sad cow. There was only one thing wrong with his face and that was the ears. Danny's ears were big and yellow, and they stood out at right angles to his head. From the front they looked as though they had been screwed into his skull, and one had been screwed in a lot further than the other. His straight carrot hair was very long and thick and brushed back over his head. When he scuffled about on his bandy arms with that half hundredweight dangling from his teeth, his mop opened downwards off his scalp as though it was

on a hinge, and bumped along the cobble-stones. He was very
proud of his teeth. He thought so much of them he never showed
them to anyone. Nobody ever saw Danny grinning.

My own line was that special cube I had invented to keep
the flies off the meat. I used to soften down a few candles and
shape the grease into dices with my fingers. Then I put one or
two of these white dices on a cut of meat on my trestle in the
middle of the market crowds. There were always plenty of fat
flies and bluebottles buzzing about in those markets, what with
the boiled sweet stalls and the horse-droppings, but you never
saw one perching on my meat with the white cubes on it. This
wasn't because the flies didn't like candle-grease but because
under the meat-plate I had a saucer of paraffin oil.

One night Danny and I were sitting on the bed in our lodging house. The place was filthy and lousy and we were catching
bugs on our needles off the walls and roasting them to death one
by one in the candle flame. Danny was bitter. The fair had
finished but the farmers had kept their hands on their ha'pennies. And the weather was bad, very wet and gusty and cold all
the time. Danny said we were pioneers. He said these farmers
were savages, they didn't care about having filthy teeth, or
eating their food fly-blown. He was very down-hearted. He
hadn't had much to eat for a few days and between the noisy
bursting of the bugs his empty belly crowed. I was down-
hearted too. We had to get money from somewhere to pay for
our lodgings and a seat in the horsebrake drawing out of town
the next morning. I asked Danny to come out into the town to
see what we could pick up but he wouldn't. At first he said it was
too cold. Then he said he had got to darn his tights and his
stockings. In the end I went by myself.

The town had been newly wetted with another downpour
and Danny was right about the cold. As I walked up the dark
empty main street I could feel the wind blowing into the holes
in my boots. Everywhere was closed up and silent and deserted.
I looked in at the Bell and the Feathers and the Glyndŵr, but
they were all empty. Then from the swing door of the Black

Horse I saw inside a big broad-shouldered man sitting down by himself in the bar. Apart from him the bar was deserted. He was by the fire and his back was towards me. I knew bumming a drink out of him would be as easy as putting one hand in the other. I knew this because he had a red wig on coming down over the collar of his coat, and a man who wears a wig is lonely.

On the table in front of the man I could see a glass of whisky and in his hand was a little black book. He was singing a hymn out of it in Welsh. It was sad, a funeral hymn, but very determined. I stood by the door of the empty bar and listened. The Horse was small and gloomy inside. I wondered if I would go in. The man seemed huge in the neck and across the shoulders, and every time he moved all the flesh on him seemed to begin to tremble. If he kept dead still he stopped trembling. I went in past him and stood the other side of the table by the fire.

When I got round to the front of this man something snapped like a carrot inside me. His face was hideous. The flesh of it looked as though it had been torn apart into ribbons and shoved together again anyhow back on to the bones. Long white scars ran glistening through the purple skin like ridges of gristle. Only his nose had escaped. This was huge and dark and full of holes, it curved out like a big black lump of wood with the worm in it. He was swarthy, as though he was sitting in a bar of shadow, and I looked up to see if perhaps a roof-beam had come between him and the hanging oil-lamp lighting the bar. There wasn't a hair on him, no moustache or eyebrows, but his wig was like the bright feathers of a red hen. It started a long way back, half way up his scalp, and the gristly scars streamed down over his forehead and cheekbones from under it. He had a tidy black suit on and a good thick-soled boot with grease rubbed in. The other leg was what looked like a massive iron pipe blocked up at the end with a solid wooden plug. It came out on to the hearth from the turn-up of his trousers.

It is best to tell the tale when you haven't got any cash to put on the counter. When I began to talk to him by the fire I tucked my feet under the settle and said I was a salesman. Although Danny and I could put all our belongings in a to-bacco-box, I soon had a fine range of second-hand goods for sale. The man closed his little book to listen. He told me he was Jordan, man-servant to the old doctor of the town. I took a polished piece of a rabbit's backbone out of my waistcoat pocket and passed it over to him. It looked like a small cow's skull, complete with horns. He examined it slowly, trembling all the time. He had huge soft hands and his finger-nails were as green as grass. I told him he could keep it. He called for whisky for both of us.

As I drank my whisky I enjoyed thinking what I had for sale. I had a little harmonium, portable, very good for Welsh hymns, perfect except for a rip in the bellows; a new invention that would get a cork out of a bottle – like that!; a nice line in leather purses, a free gift presented with each one – a brass watch-key, number eight, or a row of glass-headed pins; a pair of solid leather knee-boots, just the thing for him because they were both for the same leg. The man's eyes were small, they looked half closed up, and he watched me hard without moving them all the time. In the heat of the fire a strong smell came off him. It was a damp clinging smell, clammy, like the mildewed corner of some old church, up there behind the organ where they keep the bier. At last he bent forward and held his smashed face close to mine. I stopped talking. He trembled and said softly, 'I am interested in buying only one thing.'

Somehow I felt mesmerised, I couldn't say anything. I am not often like that. I lifted my eyebrows.

Jordan didn't answer. His little eyes slid round the empty bar. Then he moved his lips into a word that staggered me. I stared at him. For a minute by the blazing bar fire I went cold as clay. He nodded his head and made the same mouthing of his smashed face as before. The word he shaped out was, 'Corpses'.

There was dead silence between us. The clock in the bar echoed loudly, like a long-legged horse trotting down an empty street. But I let my face go into a twist and I squeezed a tear into the end of my eye. I crossed myself and offered the serving man the body of my brother. I had buried him, I remembered, a week ago come tomorrow.

Jordan took his hat and stick out of the corner. The stick was heavy, with a lot of rope wound round it, and the black hat had a wide brim. When he stood up he was like a giant rising above me. He was much bigger even than I thought. He looked down hard at the little bone I had given him and then threw it on the back of the fire. We went out into the street. As we walked along, his iron leg bumped on the pavement and made a click-clicking noise like a carried bucket. He would show me where to bring the corpse and I was to come between midnight and daybreak.

We walked together out of the town into the country. It was pitch dark and soon the way was through wet fields. It was still cold but I didn't feel it any more. Jordan had this peg leg but he was big, and I sweated keeping up with him. He trembled all the time as he walked but his shaking didn't make you think he was weak. He was like a powerful machine going full force and making the whole throbbing engine-house tremble to the foundations with its power. I trotted behind him breathless. He was so busy singing the Welsh burial hymn that he didn't drop a word to me all the way.

At last we came to a gate across the lane we were following. There was a farm-house beyond it, all in darkness. Jordan stopped singing and shouted, twice. There was no reply. He started singing again. He poised himself on his iron leg and his walking stick and gave the gate a great kick with his good foot. It fell flat. We found ourselves going at full speed across a farmyard. A heavy sheepdog ran out of the shadows barking and showing a fringe of teeth. He looked huge and fierce enough to tear us in pieces. Jordan didn't pause and I kept close behind him. The dog changed his gallop into a stiff-legged prowl, and he filled his throat with a terrible snarl. Then suddenly he sprang straight at Jordan's throat. As he rose in the air Jordan hit him a ringing crack on the head with his stick. He used both hands to bring it down. The dog dropped to the pebbles of the yard passing a contented sigh. He didn't move again. Jordan put his good foot on him and brought the stick down on his head again and again. He went on doing this, his sad hymn getting louder and louder, until the dog's brains came out. I went cold in my sweat to hear him. At last he wiped the handle of the stick in the grass of the hedge and went on down the lane, singing.

We came in sight of the lights of a big house. 'That's the place,' he said. 'Bring it round to the back door. Good night.'

He went off into the darkness like a giant in his broad-brimmed hat. I wiped the sweat off my head. After he had disappeared I could hear his hymn and his leg clicking for a long time. His hymn was slow and sad, but it didn't make me unhappy at all. It frightened the life out of me.

On the way back to the town I kicked the dead dog into the ditch.

Danny never let his job slide off his back. As I climbed up the stairs of our lodging house I came face to face with two eyes watching me through the upright bars of the top landing banister. It was Danny dawdling about on his hands, practising. I had a lot of trouble persuading him to be a corpse. All he had to do was pretend to be dead and to let me and the black-man on the landing below carry him out to the doctor's house. Then when we were paid and everybody in the house was asleep he could get out of one of the downstairs windows. We would be waiting for him. We could leave the town by the first brake in the morning. It was safe as houses. Nothing could go wrong. At last Danny agreed.

At midnight the three of us set out for Jordan's house. We were me, Danny and Marky. Marky was a half-caste cheapjack, a long thin shiny man the colour of gunmetal, selling fire-damaged remnants and bankrupt stock and that. He used to

dribble and paw you at close quarters but he would do anything you asked him for tuppence or thruppence. We walked
through the fields carrying a rolled up sack and my trestle
until we came in sight of the house Jordan had shown me. Danny
stripped to his coms under a tree and hid his clothes. He put on
an old cream-flannel nightgown Marky had brought out of
stock. Then we sewed him in the sack and put him on the planks
of my trestle. It was pitch dark and cold, with the small rain
drizzling down again as fine as pepper.

The doctor's house was all in darkness. We went round to
the little pointed wooden door at the back of the garden. I
whispered to Danny to ask if he was all right. There were two
answers, Danny's teeth chattering and the uproar of dogs howling and barking inside the garden. I had never thought about
dogs. What were we going to do?

At once I heard the click of the leg the other side of the wall
and Jordan's voice speaking. 'Down, Farw. Down, Angau,' he
growled. The narrow pointed door was thrown open, and
suddenly we saw Jordan. He was stripped naked to the half
and he had left off his wig. He looked so huge, so powerful and
ugly in the doorway, with his swelling nose and his fleshy body
all slashed, I almost let go of our load with fright. And behind
him the hounds, three of them, black and shaggy and big as
ponies, yelped and bayed and struggled to get past him to
attack us. Jordan spoke sharply to them and at last we were able
to carry Danny into the garden. He was as light on the boards
as a bag of hay. Jordan spoke only to the dogs. He made a sign
and led us hobbling along the pebble path across the yard
towards some dark out-houses. The three hounds paced whining
beside us, sniffing all the time at the sack and spilling their
dribble.

The room we went into smelt like a stable. It was dim and
empty but there was an oil lamp hanging from a nail in a low
beam. We laid Danny across some feed-boxes under this lamp.
Jordan stood back by the stable door with the whimpering dogs
while we were doing it, watching us all the time. I could feel

his eyes burning into my back. His skin was very dark and his chest bulged up into big paps resting above his powerful folded arms. But all his body was torn with terrible wounds like his face. Long shining scars like the glistening veins you see running through the rocks of a cliff-face spread in all directions over his flesh. His bald head had a large dome on it and that was covered with scars too. His whole body gleamed down to his waist, the drizzle had given him a high shine like the gloss of varnish.

We left Danny lying on the boards across the feed-boxes and came back up to the door to ask for our money. Jordan didn't reply. Instead he took a large clasp-knife out of the pocket in the front of his trousers and opened it. Then, ordering the dogs to stay, he went past us and bumped over to where Danny was lying in his sack. He seemed to take a long time to get there. There was dead silence. As he went from us we could see a black hole in his back you could put your fist into. My skin prickled. Marky's eyes rolled with the dogs sniffing him and he began to paw the air. I looked round and saw a hay-fork with a stumpy leg in the corner. Jordan turned round under the lamp and looked back at us. The blade of the open knife trembled in his hand. He turned again and cut open the sewing in the sack above Danny's face. I could hardly breathe. Danny was so white under the hanging lamp I thought he was really dead. My hair stirred. Danny's teeth showed shining in his open mouth, and in the lamplight falling right down upon them the whites of his half-opened eyes glistened. He was pale and stiff, as if he had already begun to rot. Jordan bent over, gazing down at him with the knife in his hand, the lamp spreading a shine over the skin of his wet back. I was frightened, but if Danny's teeth chattered or his belly crowed I was willing to use that pitchfork to get us out. At last Jordan turned. He spoke for the first time.

'He is a good corpse,' he said.
'He is my brother,' I told him.
'Where did you get him from?'
'I dug him up.'

He nodded. He left the knife open on the feed-box and came over to us. Putting his hand again into his front pocket he brought out a large lump of wadding. This he opened and in the middle lay three gold sovereigns. He passed the coins over to me with his huge trembling hands and motioned us out roughly. He went back and blew out the oil-lamp and we left Danny alone there in the darkness. Jordan locked the stable door and the hounds trotted round us growling as we left the garden through the little door.

'Good night,' said Jordan.

'Good night, brother,' I said.

We walked about in the fields, trying to keep warm, waiting for the time to go back to get Danny out. Marky had gone icy cold. I was worried, especially about those dogs. I wished I had a drop of drink inside me. When we thought everything would be quiet again we went back to see if it was safe to give Danny the whistle. I threw my coat over the bottle-glass stuck on top of the garden wall and climbed up. I could see a candle lit in a downstairs window of the doctor's house and by its light Jordan moved about inside the room in his nightshirt and nightcap. Presently his light disappeared and all was in darkness.

An owl in a tree close by started screeching. Marky was frightened and climbed up on to the garden wall to be near me. There was no sign of Jordan's dogs in the garden. It was bitterly cold up there on top of the wall without our coats on. The wind was lazy, it went right through us instead of going round. It had stopped raining again. There was a moon now but it was small and a long way off, very high up in the sky, and shrunken enough to go into your cap.

We waited a long time shivering and afraid to talk. Marky's eyes were like glass marbles. At last I saw something moving in the shadows by the stable. My heart shot up hot into my throat. Marky caught hold of me trembling like a leaf. A figure in white began to creep along the wall. It was Danny. He must have got out through one of the stable windows. I whistled softly to him and at that there was uproar. The three hounds came bounding across the yard from nowhere, making straight for Danny, baying and snarling like mad. I didn't know what to do for the moment with fright. The dogs were almost on top of him. Danny sprang on to his hands and began trotting towards them. His black legs waved in the air and his nightshirt fell forward and hung down to the ground over his head. The dogs stopped dead when they saw him. Then they turned together and galloped away into the shadows howling with fright. When Danny reached the wall we grabbed him firmly by the ankles and pulled him up out of the garden at one pluck. We were not long getting back to our lodging-house. The next morning we paid our landlord and the brake driver with one of the sovereigns we had had off Jordan.

I didn't have any luck. All the rest of the summer it was still wet and there were hardly any flies. I tried selling elephant charms, very lucky, guaranteed, but the harvest failed and in the end I couldn't even give them away. Danny got thinner and thinner and more quiet. He was like a rush. He had nothing to say. There never was much in his head except the roots of his hair. Having been a corpse was on his mind. And he was like a real corpse to sleep with, as cold as ice and all bones. He lost interest even in standing on his hands.

We visited a lot of the towns that held fairs but without much luck. One market day we were sitting in a coffee tavern. It was a ramshackle place built of wooden planks put up for the market day in a field behind the main street. The floor was only grass and the tables and benches stood on it. You could get a plate of peas and a cup of tea there cheap. Danny didn't care about food now even when we had it. Because it was market day this coffee tavern was crowded. It was very close inside, enough to make you faint, and the wasps were buzzing everywhere. All the people around us were jabbering Welsh and eating food out of newspapers.

Presently, above the noise, I heard a bumping and clicking sound in the passage. I felt as though a bath-full of icy water had shot over me inside my clothes. I looked round but there was no way of escape. Then I heard the funeral hymn. In a minute Jordan was standing in the entrance of the coffee tavern. He was huge, bigger than ever, a doorful. In one hand was his roped-up stick and in the other his black hymn-book. His broad-brimmed hat was on his head, but instead of his wig he had a yellow silk handkerchief under it with the corners knotted. He stopped singing and stood in the doorway looking round for an empty seat. A man from our table just then finished his peas and went out. Jordan saw the empty place and hobbled in. We couldn't escape him. He came clicking through the eating crowd like an earthquake and sat down at our table opposite us.

At first I didn't know what to do. Danny had never seen Jordan and was staring down at the grease floating on his tea. I tried to go on leading the peas up to my mouth on my spoon but I could hardly do it. Jordan was opposite, watching me. He could see I was shaking. I pretended to fight the wasps. I could feel his bright bunged-up eyes on me all the time. He put his arms in a ring on the table and leaned over towards me. I was spilling the peas in my fright. I couldn't go on any longer. I lowered my spoon and looked at him. He was so hideous at close quarters I almost threw up. The big black block of his nose reached out at me, full of worm-holes, and the rest of his face looked as though it had been dragged open with hooks. But he was smiling.

'Jordan,' I said, although my tongue was like a lump of cork. 'Mr. Jordan.'

He nodded. 'You've come back,' he said. 'Where have you been keeping?'

The whole coffee tavern seemed to be trembling with his movements. I felt as though I was in the stifling loft of some huge pipe-organ, with the din coming out full blast and all the hot woodwork in a shudder. His question had me stammering. I told him I had been busy. My business kept me moving, I travelled about a lot. The wooden building around me felt suffocating, airless as a glasshouse. I glanced at Danny. He looked as though he had been tapped and all his blood run off. Even his yellow ears had turned chalky.

Jordan nodded again, grinning his terrible grin. 'The chick born in hell returns to the burning,' he said. All the time he watched me from under the front knot of his yellow handkerchief. He ignored Danny altogether. His eyes were small, but they looked as though each one had had a good polish before being put into his head.

'Our bargain was a good one,' he went on, still smiling. 'Very good. It turned out well.'

I was afraid he would hear my swallow at work, it sounded loud even above the jabbering. 'I am glad,' I said, 'I did my best. I always do my best.'

'My master was pleased,' he said. He leaned further forward and beckoned me towards him. I bent my head to listen and his wooden nose was up touching my ear. 'A splendid corpse,' he whispered. 'Inside, a mass of corruption. Tumours and malignant growths. Exactly what my master needed. Cut up beautifully, it did.'

There was a loud sigh from Danny. When I turned to look at him he wasn't there. He had gone down off his bench in a heap on the grass. People all round got up from their tables and crowded round. Some of them waved their arms and shouted. 'Give him air,' they said, 'he's fainted. Give him air.' For a minute I forgot all about Jordan. I told the people Danny was my friend. They carried him out of the coffee tavern and laid him on the grass at the side of the road. 'Loosen his neck,' somebody said, and his rubber breast and collar were snatched off showing his black coms underneath. The crowd came on like flies round jam. At last Danny opened his eyes. Someone brought him a glass of water out of the coffee tavern. He sat up, bowed his shoulders and put his hands over his face as though he was crying. I spotted something then I had never noticed before. There was a big bald hole in his red hair at the top

of his head. He looked sickly. But before long he could stand
again. I pushed his breast and collar into my pocket and took
him back to our lodging house. I looked round but I couldn't
see Jordan at all in the crowd. Danny was in bed for a week. He
was never the same again. For one thing if he cut himself shaving
he didn't bleed. The only thing that came out of the cut was a
kind of yellow water.

Before the year was out I had buried Danny. It was wild
weather and he caught a cold standing about half-naked in his
tights in the fairs and markets. He took to his bed in our lodgings.
Soon he was light-headed and then unconscious. Every night I
sat by him in our bedroom under the roof with the candle lit
listening to his breathing.

One night I dropped off to sleep in the chair and he woke me
up screaming. He dreamt Jordan was trying to chop his hands
off to make him walk on the stumps. I was terrified at the noise
he made. The candle went out and the roar of the wind
sawing at the roof of the house was deafening. My heart was
thumping like a drum as I tried to relight the candle. I
couldn't stop Danny screaming. A few minutes later he
died with a yell. Poor Danny. Being a corpse was too much
for him. He never struggled out from under the paws of his
memories.

The next night the man from the parish came. He asked me
if I wasn't ashamed to bury my friend like that. He meant that
Danny hadn't had a shave for a week. In the candle-light he
had a bright copper beard and he wasn't quite so much like a
cow. When the man had gone I started to shave the corpse. It
was hard doing it by candle-light. High up on the cheek-bone
I must have done something wrong, I must have cut him,
because he opened one of his eyes and looked hard at me with it.
I was more careful after that. I didn't want to open that vein
they say is full of lice.

The morning of the funeral I borrowed a black tie off our landlord. I bummed a wreath on strap. It was very pretty. It was a lot of white flowers on wires made into the shape of a little arm-chair. In the bars of the back was a card with the word 'Rest' on it done in forget-me-nots. Danny always liked something religious like that.

There was nobody in the funeral except the parson and me and two gravediggers. It was a bad day in autumn and very stormy. The long grass in the graveyard was lying down smooth under the flow of the wind. There were some willow trees around the wall all blown bare except for a few leaves sticking to the thin twigs like hair-nits. The parson in his robes was a thin man but he looked fat in the wind. As he gabbled the service the big dried-up leaves blown along the path scratched at the gravel with webbed fingers, like cut-off hands. I wanted to run away. When Danny was in the earth the gravediggers left. The parson and I sang a funeral hymn. The wind was roaring. As we were singing I heard another voice joining in in the distance. It was faint. I had been waiting for it. I didn't need to look round. I knew the sound of the voice and the clicking leg. They came closer and closer. Soon the voice was deafening, the sad hymn roaring like a waterfall beside me. Jordan came right up and stood between me and the parson, touching me. For shaking he was like a giant tree hurling off the storm. His little black book was in his hand. Even in the wind I could smell the strong mouldiness that came off him, clammy as grave-clay. He was bigger than ever. The brim of his black hat was spread out like a roof over my head. As he stood beside me he seemed to be absorbing me. He put his arm with the night-stick in his hand around my shoulders. I felt as though I was gradually disappearing inside his huge body. The ground all around me melted, the path began to flow faster and faster past my feet like a rushing river. I tried to shout out in my terror. I fainted.

When I came round the parson was beside me. We were sitting on the heap of earth beside Danny's open grave. I was as wet as the bed of the river with fright. When I spoke to the parson about Jordan he humoured me. That was a fortnight ago. Yesterday when I cut myself shaving I didn't bleed. All that came out of the cut was a drop or two of yellow water. I won't be long now. I am finished. I wouldn't advise anybody to try crossing Jordan.

THE BOY IN THE BUCKET

Dockery-crick – dockery-crick, went the clock in the silence.

Outside the chapel windows the Sabbath-silent sun deluged morning over the valley. Only a few clouds, woolly puffs of sunlit willowherb, floated by on the blue. On the opposite side of the *cwm* a great whale-browed mountain rose up bedecked and glittering into the sunlight. It had the fascination for Ceri of a vast velvet monster risen green from the lumber-room of sea-bottom, bearing upon its brow grove-growths and out-cropping rocks and rows of cottages. Sunday after Sunday, morning and evening, he watched it from his seat, in silence as now, or with the shameless shouting of the rooks in his ears. But today he was not able to pay so much attention to it as usual. He was afraid Roderick the policeman was going to call at his house with a Blue Paper.

The service was bound to start soon now. The six black-clad daughters of Penffordd were already in, they had swept up the aisle in their silk-swishing mourning and, like one man, stuck their foreheads to the hymn-book ledge. Richards the Stoning in the side-seats was getting restless. He was an old man with white hair and beard, but the thick hairs in his ears were brown as though he had been smoking through them. He stretched his legs in impatience and the splitting timber of his pew-back crack-cracked sharp as pistol shots in the silence. Mrs. Rees the Bank in her fox-furs was worried by a fly. From the little gallery behind came a loud cackle like trucks shunting, and Ceri knew without looking back that old Bara-chaws the roadman was up there, clearing the metallic phlegm out of his throat for the singing.

Ceri always loved the sunshine to fill up the chapel. The walls, washed in a buttercup light, looked so clean, and the bright green paint on the gas brackets glistened with such freshness that they appeared wet. On the wall behind the pulpit a large curved ribbon with '*Duw cariad yw*' on it was painted in salmon-tin gold—'God is love.' And as Ceri was admiring the gleam of it the door beside the pulpit opened and Jones the schoolteacher led the deacons into the Big Seat. Jones was Ceri's dayschool teacher, he had scabs in his hair and he used to go behind the blackboard to pick them off. Then the preacher, a very narrow man in black and glasses, entered and went up into the pulpit. His hairless head was lacquered a heavy brown, it always took the reflection of the chapel lights on its polish, and now there was a nice ring of windows gleaming all around it. He gave out the hymn, the harmonium started and all the people stood on their feet to sing.

Ceri's mother used to sit in the front of the chapel to see that the little children gathered together there behaved themselves during the service. Because of that Ceri felt it was safe to look around a bit. Right in front of him was Hughes the *Vulcan*, old dome-head, the back of his neck glowing like a ploughed sunset. You could always rely on Hughes to sigh out loud, bored, if the sermon was poor, and this helped Ceri to know what to tell his mother about it when she questioned him after chapel. Across the aisle Mair Morgans was wearing a new lot of best clothes. Her straw hat had a ring of juicy cherries around it and on her crimson coat were large wooden buttons, round and yellow, with plaited edges like tartlets. The pew door hid the rest of her but most likely she had new shoes on too, because every now and then she would stop singing, move her hymn-book sideways and have a good peep down at her feet.

But one thought kept on worrying Ceri; what would his mother say when Roderick the policeman knocked at the front door with the summons in his hand? It drove him desperate to think of it. She made everything out to be so serious, such as being kept in after school, or swearing by accident, or breaking down in the psalm he was supposed to have learnt for the *gymanfa*. He didn't mean any harm, but she always made him feel that whatever he did was wicked. Only the other day, when they all had their heads bowed over their baked potatoes and she was asking a blessing, he and his little sister couldn't stop giggling and his mother said that was an *insult* to *Iesu Grist*. What would she say when she knew he had been playing with the O'Driscolls again and had broken the street lamp through throwing stones? He felt a sultry flush soaking his face, and just then he caught her large varnished eye full upon him, she had turned it back over her shoulder in a frown because Ceri was dreaming and had forgotten he was supposed to be singing the hymn.

When the sermon came Ceri was afraid to make sketches of the deacons so he settled down against the door of the pew to have a good worry. On the mountain opposite he could see the overhead wires that carried the bucketed colliery dirt away, and the diminishing row of trellis masts supporting them. The O'Driscolls would be on their way up the mountain now, most likely, and he wished he could be with them again. Ceri's mother preached day after day against playing with them – knowing their mother she always called them 'Ceridwen's boys' – because they were rough and bad swearers. But Ceri could see nothing wrong with them except that they never had pocket handkerchiefs. They pinched their noses with their fingers and shot it into the gutter. But they were all kind boys. Aneirin, the youngest, would take a lump of chewing-gum from behind his ear where he always kept it stuck and bite a half of it for you; Ginger Irfon would give you a go on the bar of his pink bike that had such soft tyres you felt you were riding on jubes; and Taliesin, the big one, would let you come in their gymnasium shed in the backyard any time and have a bang at the punching-ball. But Ceri's mother said he wasn't to have anything to do with them. Their mother was Welsh but their father was an Irishman, and they never went to chapel properly, only to the mission sometimes just before there was going to be a teaparty.

There was a patch of ground at the end of the O'Driscoll's row where you could kick a ball about, but you had to stop for horses and carts to pass. While they were playing football there one of the boys from down by the canal drove his horse and cart by; his job was to collect the small coal the colliers didn't want and left heaped in the lanes outside their houses. This boy was black as a sweep and dressed like a scarecrow, and his cart was falling to bits, it even had a big piece out of the rim of one of the wheels. The poor nag could hardly creep along, his back sagged like a drying-line and his harness was tied together with cord and wire.

Taliesin had picked up the ball they were playing with, a soccer case stuffed with newspaper, but the horse was so long creeping across the patch that he became impatient. 'Come on, Small-coal,' he shouted. 'Get a move on.'

'Shut your blower, snobby-nose,' the boy on the cart answered.

'Shut your blower yourself,' Tally shouted back, 'or I'll come and shut it for you.'

The boy snatched up a handful of small-coal off the cart behind him and flung it point-blank in Tally's face. Then the stone-throwing began. Ceri's stone went right through the street lamp they used as a goal-post and they all ran away. They had a last glimpse of the small-coal boy; he had fallen off the cart and was being dragged across the ground on his back with his heel caught in the harness.

Ceri was terrified with the memory of it. What was going to happen? Up there in the pulpit, behind the golden edges of the Bible, the minister was preaching a sermon that kept the *Vulcan* silent. The light was coming through from the windows behind the preacher, it filled one of the thick pebbles of his glasses and swelled it up into the size of an enormous glowing eye. Oh dear, oh dear, what could he do?

Outside, across the valley, the bright sunlight poured down on the monstrous velvet scalp of the mountain, with the file of dressmakers' dummies going up over it, and the overhead wires sagging across it between them like pulled-out chewing-gum. Because it was Sunday the buckets were empty and stationary. It was almost time now for Miss Rees to tap Ceri on the shoulder from the seat behind and for him to put his hand carelessly on the back of the pew to receive his peppermint.

Life seemed so dangerous to him, like a large black savage dog in the road, and all he wanted was to creep by unnoticed. Oh, how he wished he was away. How lovely to go up over the mountain now, to be up there in the air and the sunlight for ever. To be a stander in a Sunday-still muck-bucket, to hang over the *cwm*, a trapezist, two hundred feet above the river. Over his head, not very far off, he imagined the blue sky with a limpid bloom of illumination upon it, and the snowy cushions and pillowings floating there, the silken bulgings of the sunlit shadow-casters, the radiant clouds. Grasping tightly the thick bars going overhead to the wheels, he looked over the edge of the bucket. Everything below was placid and motionless. The whole valley lay green beneath him like an apron held out for catching. There was the river in the middle, glittering, from so high above, in a silvery vein. There on either side of it the slopes of the mountains glowed in the sunlight, the great whale-headed promontory was dimmed as the cloud shadows passed over it, and its grass blazed bright green again in the sun when their darkness had gone, like a heap of embers with the bellows blowing them. Further down the valley, where the pits were, a long solitary bow of black smoke curved out of a pitstack. Right beneath him he could see his village, standing to attention in fourteen rows of yellow brick and whitewash; and his own tidy little street, Ugain Tŷ, remote in the hillside trees, its chimneys all boiling fast into the morning like the spouts of a row of kettles. The chapel gleamed beautiful on the slope, snow-white and long-windowed. Nothing moved except Griffith's coal-black mare, a speck stirring on the bright green slope. And then, just beneath him, a flock of small birds went by in the breeze, their wings were shut, and they swam like a swarm of fish through the clear air.

He felt with surprise the nudge of Miss Rees. Sliding his hand along the back of the pew he received his peppermint.

A martin shot up to the chapel window and fell abruptly away, its wing tearing the morning with a lateral stab. The wheels overhead squealed. The bucket began to move. A little engine, under a mop of steam, burst round the curve of the valley. Ceri climbed with a rapture of increasing speed the slope of the mountain. Great lights seemed to fall upon him, as though he stood upon a vast stage. He was away. He heard his departure heralded by hooters and birdsong, his bucket swayed in delight, sailing rapidly like a great bird over the belfries of the trees.

'Goodbye, cottages,' he called. 'Goodbye over-tidy Ugain Tŷ; goodbye little valley; goodbye spreading fan of valleys; goodbye little chapel; goodbye Mam, Dad and obligation, I give you all farewell and a big kiss. In my bucket of salmon-tin gold I leave you, it is my saviour. I have enhanced it with poppies and elder-blooms, badged it bolder than diplomats, I have decorated its edges with paper lace. Goodbye Roderick, goodbye Blue Paper, up the mountain I go in the shaken-down showers of light and the hullabaloo of birdsong. My troubles I leave behind, my heart has a long wing on each side of her, her feathery breast is breeze-borne, she is buoyant in her iron bucket. I am the lord of the bucket, and I have a lung full of laughing. I am the bucket-borne boy, I am the boy in the bucket, I am bucketed boy. I am on the heights, the world is blotted out, the sun, the all-seer, sees only me; all the valley, all the world below is hidden under the long rhomboids of smokes. The radiance of upper air enveloping my bucket is bright, but pale, like bedroom gaslight. The great swans of joy and illumination beat up around me, Oh, milky majestic thunder, Oh, rhythmic throbbing snow, Oh, compounded flakes and plumage of snowstorms of brightness. Lead me on. Lead me on to my dirty auntie – somewhere I have her – and my cousins of chaos, unreproved; to the houseful of children spotted like wall-paper, to the white mice in swarms and the great flocks of pigeons, to the house of indifference and joy. Lead me on to the wise, the wished-for and the wonderful.

'One of my cousins is the same age as I am, but he never gets out of bed to go to school in the morning. When the teachers scold him my auntie goes up to school and shouts at them, striking them on the behind with her umbrella. My cousin smells of stale tobacco. He has long corduroy trousers with baggy knees and brass railway-buttons everywhere. His face is enchanting and completely covered with warts, it has a crust of yellow warts laid all over it, each one no bigger than a pinhead. All day long we are down the beach in the beautiful weather, we spend our time rolling a heavyweight gambo-wheel about in the fine sand. My cousin knows many dirty songs which he sings sweetly. We find a heap of cherries swept into the roadside and we eat them instead of going home to dinner. My cousin spits and if it falls on the knees of his corduroys he doesn't wipe it off. I sleep with him the first night, and the second night, and by the third night I am lousy.

'It is just after teatime when I arrive. My auntie is kind and she gives me a cup of port to drink. She is a stout woman. Her fat arms are the inflamed shiny colour of rhubarb, but her nails are black. Her hair is coming down. She smiles all the time, and all the time she smiles she draws a lip down over a bunch of black teeth. Her blouse comes out around her waist. She never takes her apron off in the afternoon. After dinner she piles the dirty dishes back in the cupboard, and goes out to talk over the wall with the woman next door from the steps of the *dubliw*.

'The old granny sits by the fire every day with her chin on her stick. She is very old and hairy everywhere. If you speak to her she parts the hair hanging over her eyes with her fingers to see who it is. She is in her second childhood and my cousin asks me to come and watch him teasing her.

' "How old are you now, Mamgu?" he says to her. "Tell us now, honestly, when will you be two hundred?"

' "I am not old," she cackles, "I am not old, I tell you."

' "Come on, Mamgu, tell us about the battle of Waterloo. You can remember that, can't you?"

' "I am not old," she shrieks at him, "I am not old." She puts the yellow claws of her hands on her chest. "Feel me, if you don't believe, feel me by here, I am like a girl." My cousin looks at me and laughs. She waves her walking stick at him in temper. "Go away," she says, "or I'll go home to my father and mother. You naughty boy, you."

'Just then my auntie comes in from the backyard. "Now then," she says, "stop teasing your grannie. And wipe your nose." My cousin draws his sleeve across it.

'On Sunday afternoon my auntie goes to bed with my uncle. My cousin and I don't go to Sunday school. We play ludo on the mat in the middle room where my uncle has left his flannel shirt on a coat-hanger. Suddenly there is a loud crash and the leg of the bed comes through the ceiling.

'My uncle is a tall man and very jolly. He hardly ever wears a jacket or a collar and tie, he is about the house in broken boots and an open waistcoat. There is a clear green stud-stain on the front of his neck. His face is like frayed fibre because he always wants a shave, and he has an oily quiff buttered down on his forehead. He does light hauling. His cart is painted all over a light purple, shafts and wheels and all. My cousin says you could tell he had pinched the paint for it, because nobody would *buy* paint that colour. His horse has prominent bones, and such a bent back you feel you want to pull his tail hard to straighten it. My uncle keeps a stub of a pencil behind his ear and writes notes on his matchbox. To save money he smokes ferns and then all the children go out to play coughing. He is the best everything where they live. He was the one who fired the very last bullet before the hooters put a stop to the war. When he hasn't been to the pub he sits downhearted opposite the grannie by the fire, and then my auntie gives him beer-money to get drunk.

'One night we are all having supper in the kitchen. The oil-lamp is lit and the six spotty children are around the table. It has been too wet for light hauling and my uncle has been in the Beehive all day. He is happy and he makes us all laugh. Suddenly we see a big black rat running across the shelf of the dresser, and everybody is excited. My uncle dashes from the table and is just in time to hold the rat fast behind a big willow-pattern meat-dish. The creature struggles but he cannot get away. My uncle holds him with one hand, and with the other fumbles the two-pronged carving-fork out of the knife drawer. We all sit fascinated, wondering what he will do. Gradually he allows the rat to squeeze out from behind the dish, and then with a sudden jab pins him to the wall with the fork. The fork goes right through the rat's body and into the soft plaster. The rat screams loudly for a bit and then dies. My uncle takes him by the tail and throws him on the fire.

'Every night my cousin and I go to bed in our shirts and we do not clean our teeth. In the kitchen, behind the old grannie, there is a smoky mirror. It must have come from somewhere else, because it has a keyhole in it. I clean the corner with my elbow and examine myself. My face is covered with a mass of rough skin like breadcrumbs, and my teeth are coloured in bands – black near the gums, then khaki, then grass-green, and a thin fringe of white at the sharp edges.

'My auntie is going to have a washing day and the kitchen is full up to the door with steam. We can just see the grannie by the fire through the swirling mists, eating gruel out of a basin with a wooden spoon and spitting the hard bits all over the floor. My auntie sits down at the table with us, tugging the bacon rinds through her broken teeth.

'Suddenly there is a sharp knock at the back door. When my auntie opens it we see Roderick the policeman there with the Blue Paper in his hand. It is a perishing day and his face is the crimson of a fire bucket. But he is cosy, the thick soles of his boots hold him up off the cold floor, his long heavy overcoat wraps his body from the wind, and even his ears are plugged up with cotton-wool against the weather. The steam from the kitchen blows out around him as he scowls in the doorway and points in my direction with a white woollen glove. I am terrified. I have been so happy and indifferent I have forgotten all about the Blue Paper. Roderick shouts it is for me. My auntie snatches it off him and comes back with it through the steam to the table. I begin to sob.

' "Don't you worry, *bach*," she says to me. "I'll show you what I think of Roderick the policeman and his summonses."

'She looks angry. She takes two slices of bread and dripping off the table, puts the Blue Paper between them and starts to chew the sandwich. Her face is red.

' "Don't you worry, *bach*," she says again between chewing, "it was this Roderick that booked our Dada for carrying a bit of coal from the sidings. And for being after hours in the Beehive."

'But I am frightened. Roderick the policeman has found me. He comes angry and crimson across the kitchen. I hide in the steams and rush past him into the open.

'Oh bucket, bear me to a distance, bear me away, I cry. Oh, solid beneath me and the steamy earth far below. Oh, respite, Oh, flight, Oh, escape. I glide again over the mountain with the speed of a gliding gull, the dashing brass-clad sun accompanies me, flashing for hours across the sky. At last in the dusk I am heralded with hooters; as I go down into the valley the sun has set, the purple sunset is a long flood of plum-juice. With the stopping of the hooters my bucket comes to rest. The men far below me in the valley are going home from work. Hundreds of pit-black men begin to pour homeward along the roads of the valley. How shall I go home? I shall be suspended all night, for ever, for all eternity, above the valley, in the darkness, in the chill of the winds. I shout, I bawl, but I am too far away, no one pays any heed, all the crowds beneath me are busy with their own thoughts and homeward bound.

'I must jump. I look over the edge of my bucket and call and wave, I strip off my poppies and orders of elderboughs and cast them over the edge, but it is of no avail. Darkness comes. My tears are deep and icy cold on the floor of my bucket. I lie down in them and weep. I long for my mother and her comfort, I will return to her, I will creep under the shadows of her harsh wing.

'I throw my legs over the bucket, hang myself down by my hands over the darkening valley. The weight of my body on the rim of the bucket tips it up sideways above me. I hang in the breeze, my heart throbs. My fingers slide over the edge. When I drop where shall I land? In the trees? In Griffiths's field? Shall I be borne by the breeze to the graveyard of the chapel? I let go and fall screaming through the darkness, the trees rush past me roaring like riff-raff. . . .'

The catch on the pew door flew open under Ceri's weight and he fell with a loud crash out into the aisle. He was scarcely awake before his mother was beside him, kneeling. How beautiful she looked to his startled eyes, her black hair so lovely clustering about her ears, her large straw-brimmed hat letting the sunlight through with a new winsomeness on to her face. Never before had he smelt so sweetly the faint perfume of her, the breathed-in freshness of her presence. How lovely the chapel was, too, around her, so clean, so purified in the sun, filled up with the clear buttercup-water of the sunlight.

Sitting outside in the porch Ceri told his mother about breaking the street lamp and the Blue Paper. 'Ah,' she said, 'I dare say you couldn't help it.'

From the chapel behind them came the singing of the last hymn. The sun fell over the great headland opposite, and the houses on it, white-limed, looked unreal in their whiteness. Ceri went out on to the hot grass and had a good look at the valley.

IT'S NOT BY HIS BEAK YOU CAN JUDGE A WOODCOCK

It was nearly midnight. There was a frosty stare to the big stars and the full moon above the farmhouse gleamed like a splash of whitewash. Not a blade or a twig moved in the frozen Nantwig fields, and the only sound was the grass cracking like cake under a pair of heavy boots. In the distance the Reverend Gwilym Nanney was coming down to the farmhouse for the second time.

Gwilym was a simple man. He spoke little. He was good at making fishing-flies from the hackles of a cock. Sometimes he mixed up the points of his sermon, but he would carry a can of milk every day to a drunkard like Jim Saer and pray with him until the beer was overcome. He gave his money away. He gave away his jacket to Theo the tramp who came cuckooing through the parish in the spring. People marvelled at their vicar's big naily boots, and at his grey flannel shirt, just like their own, when he took off his coat to help with the hay of a widow, or a farmer gone into the decline. Gwilym was tall, but on his large bones no flesh had ever found a resting-place. He had the long chin, the bulging chest and the lifted shoulders of the asthmatic. From the middle of his white face the cold gristle of his nose pointed sharply up, the tip of it nibbled at the air all the time he was speaking. To visit Nantwig in the freezing weather he was wearing his round hat and his black overcoat down to his boots.

He tramped over the crust of the field and there at last, in a bowl full of trees, the light of the farmhouse shone. The whole glitter of a lake came flooding into Gwilym's moon-wet eyes. His hump of a chest wheezed, but his long and knock-kneed legs moved faster. During the last three weeks an idea had entered his mind like something green brought by a far-off pigeon. When he reached the middle of the farmyard he stood a moment under the oak tree, watching the smoke coiling out of the farmhouse chimney like a brandished rope, and thinking of what had happened in that house on his last visit. But he was clear now as to what he should do, and he would do it.

It was three weeks since the last time Gwilym had been called to Nantwig. That night, when he went into the house, he saw that the big iron double bed had been moved down into the middle of the kitchen and a great furnace of a fire stoked up in the chimney. An oil-lamp, the flame turned low in the frosted globe, was placed on the window-sill, and by its light he caught a glimpse of Phoebe Harris, the saffron-faced wife of Nantwig, peeping out at the doorway that led into the parlour. But at the sound of his boots on the kitchen flags she disappeared, and soon her stockinged feet could be heard on the ceiling boards low above his head. Gwilym took off his round hat and placed it on the brass bed-knob, where a pair of cord breeches were hung up by the braces. Then he stood gripping the bars at the foot of the bed and slowly recovering his breath.

There facing him, propped up by the pillows, a sullen look on his big red face, was Ahab Harris, Nantwig, wearing a frayed nightshirt of red flannel. Ahab, a heavy man, had pitched into the stack-yard off the roof of the stable and was dying in full flesh. But Gwilym could still feel blazing through the bedrails the bullying furnace of Ahab's strength, the power that comes from a gigantic frame, a bull's bellow and a bulging nose-bone. Ahab's fleshy face, through which whisky had driven a mass of crimson pathways, was still fiery red, the skin looked hot enough to crack open and let the flames inside blaze out. The front of his head was bald, but half-way up the scalp a torrent of thick black hair gushed out and fell behind him. He watched Gwilym with close-together eyes, too small for his huge head, while his black eyebrows, a pair of thick furry wings, shot up and down all the time like the brows of a monkey. As

Gwilym watched him in silence a purring sound came out of him like the buzz of a huge cat snoring.

What was in the heart of this Ahab, Gwilym wondered, this mocker, this flagrant adulterer, this drinker for whom there was often not room enough on the roads? Ahab was as worldly a man as any between heaven and floor, carnal and violent, never would he put his shoulder under the ark, never ponder the unsearchable riches, never once of a Sunday had he sought the lake-bank of the Means. What could he want? When Gwilym had got enough breath into his lungs the tip of his nose began its restless scribble against the air of the kitchen as he spoke.

'Good-night, Ahab Harris,' he said. 'You wanted me.'
Ahab blinked out at him.

'Yes,' he answered in his arrogant voice. 'That's right. I want to talk to you.'

'What's the matter?' Gwilym asked.

'I was fastening some loose tiles on the stable roof and I fell into the yard. Nothing serious.'

Gwilym nodded and the heavy, cunning brick-skinned face stared back at him. 'You look well,' Gwilym said.

'Why not?' Ahab answered. He grinned. 'In a week from now I'll be in town with the chestnut mare under my thighs again.'

There was a pause. Ahab spat at the fire and it boiled on the bars. Suddenly he scowled at Gwilym.

'Don't you think now, Nanney,' he said, sullen and threatening, 'from what I am going to tell you, that I am moving out of Nantwig stiff in a few days with my feet in front of me. No, no. I will stand on the graves of a good many yet, yours included. But I want you to do something for me.'

Gwilym said nothing. Then Ahab spoke about his will. He said what Phoebe and the children were to receive. They were a judgment on him and it was little. But there were some things he did not wish to put down in black and white. And he wanted Gwilym to promise that he would see these things carried out. He paused and then dropped his voice. 'Come here,' he whispered, glancing up at the ceiling, 'I want to explain to you.'

Gwilym took his hands off the sweating bars and went round to the bedside.

'You have been with religion these thirty years now, Nanney,' he said, 'and I know you are like a gunbarrel. Now listen. Although I am not clothed, yet I am in my right mind. Remember that. Across the *nant* I have five fields. You know them. Good fields. No rushes. No stones. No need to cut thistles. The best of Nantwig. They are on Twm Tircoch's side of the brook. And Twm wants to buy them. But I won't sell them to him. Do you understand, Nanney? I wouldn't give a hair of my nose to Twm Tircoch. And I refuse to sell him my fields. If I am under the big stones before Phoebe she is not to sell them to him. Now remember.'

'Thomas is a faithful churchman,' said Gwilym, 'and a good neighbour.'

'You are right,' Ahab answered, 'Twm is a faithful churchman and a good neighbour. There's nothing wrong with Twm. Only the air still goes in and out of him. Only he feels the stroke of the blood in his veins. And he sings hymns! *Yr argian fawr*, that little voice! I would sooner listen to a bandsaw. That is all. He wants my fields. I don't know why. Perhaps he thinks the railway will wish to come through them some time. Perhaps he likes the look of them under heavy hay. I won't sell them to him. I won't. But I want them sold. *Yr Israel*, yes, I want them sold. Do you understand? And do you know why? To provide for a widow. No, no, not Phoebe. Not her. My real widow. The one in Hills Terrace in town. Mrs. Watkins forty-two.'

Gwilym remembered her. He had seen her one mart day, a big purple pigeon of a woman with a mop of red hair, standing the other side of the street under the arch that leads into Hills Terrace. 'That's Ahab Nantwig's fancy,' someone said. She saw Gwilym looking at her, standing with her big hip out and her hand on it like a trollop. 'What the hell are you staring at?' she shouted across at him.

'Stoke the fire if you are cold,' Ahab called out, 'stoke the fire, man.'

Gwilym was sweating with heat and anger. His bleak nose looked warm. He picked up the big iron poker and with one blow broke the back of the fire so that it roared up the chimney. Then he came back to the bed.

'Listen,' Ahab went on. 'I want those five fields sold, and the money paid over to Mrs. Watkins. They are good fields. They will fetch a good price.'

A long and thick silence followed. Gwilym was too angry to speak. His big ears had become bright red and stiff, they shone like slices of lacquered wood. He looked up at the black ceiling near his head. It was so hot the hung bacon was sweating. What words was he to use in protest against giving to a red-haired harlot the best of Nantwig, the undercut and all the thigh slices? Five fields of ungathered hay velvet under the breeze, or ploughed red with the gulls like white pebbles upon them. All for a hard whore who wouldn't shed a tear even of gratitude. In his distress the long grey hairs brushed over his bald head fell down in a bunch, and hung tangled at the side of his face like a mass of creeper the wind has clawed by the roots off a ruin.

The bed creaked. 'Answer me,' Ahab shouted, with temper red in the webwork of veins netting his face. 'Answer me, Nanney. It's like drawing teeth to get you to speak. Do you promise or not?'

Gwilym bent his head to one side as though before the blows of a big wind. He heard the glass globe of the oil-lamp ringing at the loudness of Ahab's Welsh. How could he lay the seal of his blessing on this? But would he do more than blue himself if he fought against a hard man like Ahab? And dimly he knew what might happen to Phoebe and the children if he refused. He saw himself putting his head into a beehive but for the sake of Phoebe he nodded. 'I promise,' he said.

Ahab grunted. 'Put the belly of your hand here on my heart and swear it,' he said.

Gwilym bent forward. He placed his hand on Ahab's breast, and felt the heat blazing out through the red nightshirt as though his palm were laid against a furnace door. Ahab's huge hot hand then covered his own, glowing like a poultice, while he swore he would see the five fields were sold, but not to Twm Tircoch, and the money received for them paid over to Mrs. Watkins.

He finished, and Ahab's great, red, upholstered face was no longer sullen. He grinned. 'Good,' he said, 'and now that we've got the gambo over the hill, what about you, Nanney, what will you take as your share of the whitemeat?'

Gwilym shook his head. 'The church, Ahab Harris,' he said. 'Give something to the church.'

Ahab laughed. The bald front of his head shone like a coal-shute in the lamp-light. 'The church?' he said. 'What does the church want with money? I always thought the gospel was free.'

With considering Gwilym considered this. With his bony bare hands he picked up some of the glowing coals fallen on to the hearth and put them back on the fire. 'The gospel,' he answered at last, 'is free. But we have to pay for the paraffin oil and the sweeping brushes.'

A sound boiled up into Ahab's throat like a huge bubbling of porridge. He opened his great mouth and laughed. It was a laugh that filled the house and had in it the note of a roof-cock triumphant over many hens. Nanney the harmless, the dull as a bullock, had promised. All was well.

Nanney came out from under the oak-tree which stood in its gaiter of whitewash and went towards the farmhouse. He had finished considering. A light shone from the kitchen window. He tapped at the back door, lifted the latch and went in.

There was silence in the room. Phoebe was sitting one side of the fire and Twm Tircoch the other. The big bed had gone back upstairs and the table, with the lamp standing on it, had been returned to the middle of the room, for Ahab had been dead a fortnight. Gwilym took a stool and sat wheezing between Phoebe and Twm with his hat on his knee. Before him was a nice kitchen fire on which grew a good crop of flames like yellow bristles.

'It's a bitter night,' he gasped.

'You are right, Mr. Nanney,' said Twm in his thin voice. 'Bitter. And me thinking it was going to rain because the cat was so playful.' When Twm realized what he had done he stopped short, blushed and fell silent.

Phoebe nodded. She was a small and thin woman, her wrinkled skin seemed to be in a yellow light, as though it were catching a powerful reflection from a sheet of brass. Because of Ahab's death she was wearing a black dress but her canvas apron was still on, steaming in the heat of the fire. On her head was a gold hair-net like a soft birdcage. Gwilym could see the snow was heavy on her heart. Her face was sad and her eyes were red with weeping.

For a time the three sat in silence. Phoebe wished to ask a question but she did not know how to begin. In her embarrassment she bent forward and brushed off Nanney's shoulder a patch of brown cow-hairs left there when he had milked the cross-bred for Elin Tŷ-fri that afternoon. 'Mr. Nanney,' she said at last. 'What were his wishes?'

Gwilym paused for wind before answering. Would he be able to explain? He turned to Twm Tircoch sitting at the other side of the fire. 'Thomas,' he said, 'you wanted to buy Ahab's fields on your side of the brook. Is that right?'

Taken unawares Twm looked startled, and the colour went up his plump face to the roots of his hair. He was a big blusher of a man with a thin voice, he was shy, and he used to tell the neighbours that although he was all right with the dog he didn't know what to say to the baby. He wore a suit of bulging corduroy and the laces of his boots and all his buttons were under heavy strain. He had no collar and tie on and his stud was a brass cuff-link. Gradually his blush passed, but all over his head his untidy hair stood up, as though his scalp had been glued and he had passed through a heavy shower of craneflies.

'Yes, yes,' he said. 'And I do now. That's why I came over tonight. I hope Phoebe will give me the first chance. I will pay her a good price.'

'Ahab's wishes, Thomas,' said Gwilym, 'were that his fields on the Tircoch side of the brook were to be sold.' He paused again and looked at Phoebe. 'Phoebe,' he said, 'the night I came here to see Ahab three weeks ago, do you know what I promised Ahab?'

Phoebe shook her head. 'He never told me his business,' she said.

'I promised,' Gwilym went on, 'that I would see the five fields were sold, as the will says, but I also promised to see you did not sell them to Thomas here.'

For a moment Twm looked up in a vague way, like one suddenly conscious of a draught. Then he went red from the tight of his neckband to the roots of his hair. 'What wrong did I ever do to Ahab?' he said.

Phoebe sighed. 'When they are sold,' she said, 'what is to become of the money? I suppose it is not to come to me and the children?'

Again Gwilym looked about, thinking of words to use so that Nantwig should not fall to the dogs and the ravens. 'Phoebe,' he said, 'have you heard of Mrs. Watkins forty-two?'

Phoebe began to cry.

'She,' said Gwilym, 'is to have what is received for the five fields. I have promised it.'

There was silence in the room, except for the sobbing of Phoebe.

Twm got up to go.

'Sit down, Thomas,' said Gwilym. 'Phoebe, you must sell the fields. It is in the will.'

Phoebe nodded.

'Who will buy them?' Gwilym asked.

Phoebe raised her head. She shrugged her shoulders. 'Anyone,' she said. 'Plenty will be ready to buy them. They are good fields, as good as any in the parish.'

'Well then,' said Gwilym, wondering if this was where his plan would go under the water. 'Now listen Phoebe. Will you sell those fields to me?'

Phoebe stared. 'To you, Mr. Nanney?' she said. 'But the fields are large. And very good. And what will you be wanting five fields like that for?'

'Phoebe,' Gwilym repeated, 'will you sell them to me? All right. That is settled. I will buy the fields from you and I will give you a shilling each for them.'

'A shilling . . .' said Phoebe, and Twm began, 'But Mr. Nanney . . .'

'Will you agree?' said Gwilym. 'I will give you a shilling each for them. Remember, what you receive for the fields goes to Mrs. Watkins forty-two. If I give you a shilling each for them, that is what Mrs. Watkins will get – five shillings.'

Phoebe sat with her mouth open. Gwilym turned to Twm. Slowly he was unhooking the three-weeks old load from his heart. 'Thomas,' he said, 'you were not allowed to buy the fields off Phoebe. Will you buy them off me? For a good price?'

Twm nodded. 'And what will you do with the money, Mr. Nanney?' he asked.

'All but five shillings I shall give to Phoebe,' he said. 'Do you agree?'

Twm nodded.

'And now,' said Gwilym, wheezing suddenly, 'let us pray.'

The three stood up. Gwilym thanked God that He had made some as cunning as serpents and as harmless as doves, that out of the mouths of babes and sucklings should come forth wisdom. As he prayed he felt his legs so cold he could have sat for an hour before the fire with his feet stuffed in between the bars. He brought his prayer to a close. 'The Lord giveth and the Lord taketh away,' said Gwilym. 'Blessed be the name of the Lord.'

'Amen,' said Phoebe.

'Amen,' said Twm.